A Golden Needle

Needle

And a Silver Bullet

A Quilters Club Mystery

(Book 17)

Actual images from the Tristan Quilt

A Golden Needle

And a Silver Bullet

A Quilters Club Mystery

(Book 17)

Marjory Sorrell Rockwell

ABSOLUTELY AMAZING eBOOKS

ABSOLUTELY AMAZING eBOOKS

Manhanset House
Dering Harbor, New York 11965

bricktower@aol.com ▪ tech@absolutelyamazingebooks.com
▪ absolutelyamazingebooks.com

Library of Congress Cataloging-in-Publication Data

Rockwell, Marjorie Sorrell
A Golden Needle and a Silver Bullet
p. cm.

1. FICTION / Thrillers / Psychological
2. FICTION / Thrillers / Crime
3. CRAFTS & HOBBIES / Quilts & Quilting

ISBN: 978-1-955036-35-1, Trade Paper

January 2022

Don't needle the quilter!

Quilters Club Mysteries

By Marjory Sorrell Rockwell

**Available from
AbsolutelyAmazingEbooks.com**

A Golden Needle

Needle

And a Silver Bullet

Table of Contents

Chapter One

Greetings from the Great Beyond

The cupola atop spooky old Hoople Mansion was the perfect place to hold a séance. The big Victorian stood like a stone monolith on one of twin hillocks overlooking the Tinker Toy town of Caruthers Corners, Illinois. On the other hillock was the Perricock Museum of Science & History. Somehow it seemed odd to Maddy Madison that a superstitious ritual like a séance would be taking place only a hundred yards across a gulch from an august institution of science and reason.

Maddy didn't believe in spirits returning from the Great Beyond to communicate with the living. She knew the story: Even the wife of Harry Houdini – the famous magician who spent the last years of his life debunking spiritualists and mediums – gave up on receiving a message from him. Not even the world's greatest escape artist could escape from the grave.

Maddy's daughter Tilly had been teetering between the real world and fantasy for several years now. Tilly believed in unicorns and fairies and perhaps even dragons. And lately she had gotten into spiritualism – first, with a Ouija board and now with séances. It was unclear who she was trying to contact, in that her parents and siblings were all alive, and she'd never known any of her grandparents.

Tilly was being guided in her quest by a questionable medium who called herself Madam Flora. But according to a private investigator hired by Tilly's husband, the woman's actual name was Florence Eleanor Bashinski. Before she became affiliated with the Indiana Association of Spiritualists, she had been a manicurist.

The IAOS was headquartered at Camp Chesterfield, a spiritualist retreat just east of Indianapolis, past Pendleton and next to Anderson. Established in 1886, many sensitives – that is, mediums who are said to have the ability to communicate with spirits – live in historic cottages on the grounds of Camp Chesterfield.

Until recently, Madam Flora was one of these. However, after attaching herself to Tilly, a relationship akin to a parasitic sea lamprey latching onto a hapless fish, Flora had moved into a spare bedroom in Tilly's section of the Hoople Mansion. Tilly's husband – Mark Tidemore, mayor of Caruthers Corners – was not happy with the invasion. That's why he'd hired the p.i.

Barely a flyspeck on a roadmap, Caruthers Corners is a small town in northeast Indiana. It was founded when a westbound wagon train broke down on the banks of the Wabash River in 1829. Today, the little town is known for its watermelon crops and … well, that's about it.

Getting rid of Madam Flora had become more complicated now that Aunt Hilda and Aunt Helga – the two surviving members of the Hoople Quadruplets – had bought into Tilly's fantasy about contacting spirits. After all, Hoople Mansion belonged to them until it passed to Maddy upon their demise. The two old women might be getting dotty, but the shade of death was likely more than a decade ahead in their future.

Hilda and Helga hoped to contact their brother and sister, the two deceased quads. They giggled that it would be just like Old Times, when they were a famous foursome featured on the cover of *Time* Magazine.

Maddy's husband Beau thought this séance business was all a bunch of hooey, that Madam Flora was a money-grubbing humbug, and that her spirit guide Arthur was about as real as that big rabbit in the movie *Harvey*. He was worried about his daughter's mental health. And he wanted no part of this crazy idea about contacting dead spirits …

… until Madame Flora received a message from Col. Beauregard Hollingsworth Madison (the First), Beau's long-deceased great-grandfather. That changed everything.

The ghost told them about two murders. One occurred nearly 200 years ago, the other just a week ago. Both men died because of a quilt made in 1360.

~ ~ ~

Beauregard Hollingsworth Madison IV was a direct descendent of one of the Town Founders. Beau's antecedent, along with Jacob Abernathy Caruthers and Ferdinand Aloysius Jinks, had led that wagon train into Indian territory.

Apparently, one of the passengers – an Italian traveler listed on the manifest as Count Antonio Guicciardini – had been trying to deliver a fragment of a rare medieval quilt to a relative in San Francisco. But stranded in the new state of Indiana, the Count decided to hide the piece of quilt away until he could book passage westward.

Someone killed him trying to find the quilt fragment.

At least, that's the story the ghost told.

Chapter Two

What the Ghosts Said

"So exactly what did this spirit of your great-great-grandfather say?" Maddy asked her daughter.

Tilly Tidemore was busy sorting her bangles. She had a large collection of colorful bracelets. They ranged from ivory to glass to plastic to enamel. The colors would have done a peacock proud. She had a special glass-fronted cabinet to hold them in. Her version of a Glass Menagerie perhaps. "Why don't you ask Dad?" she said distractedly. "He heard it all."

"Your father doesn't want to talk about it," replied Maddy with a sigh.

"Why? Because he thought my séances were nonsense until he came face-to-face with an actual spirit?"

Maddy patted her daughter gently on the shoulder. "Beau will talk in his own time. His conversation with the spirit obviously shook him up. Something the ghost said."

"The ghost didn't make much sense. Just that he'd killed some Count in a duel back in 1832. And something about an old quilt."

"Tell me more, dear. I need to help your father deal with this unsettling event. So I'd like to know what went on during all that table tilting."

"Mom, there were no tilting tables. Madame Flora is the real deal, not some kind of showy fraud."

"Then tell me about it."

Tilly sat up straight, pushing her bangles aside. "In order to make contact with the Other World, Madame Flora had us sit around a table holding hands. The lights were dimmed. Everyone had to remain quiet while she summoned her spirit guide, the famous writer Arthur Conan Doyle. After a few moments he manifested himself."

"You could see him?"

"No exactly. He appeared as a glowing light up near the ceiling."

"Could you make out any of his features? His face? A shape?"

"No, Mom. Spirits are ethereal. I could only see the shimmer of his ectoplasm."

Maddy bit her tongue. She found this mumbo-jumbo hard to take seriously. "Then what happened next?" she coaxed.

"Mr. Conan Doyle –"

"Just Doyle."

"Huh?"

"Conan was actually the author's middle name. And he wasn't a Mister. He'd been knighted, so he would properly be addressed as Sir."

"Oh. He didn't introduce himself that way. He simply said, 'Cheerio, I am Mr. Conan Doyle.'"

"That should have been a clue."

Tilly looked puzzled. "A clue to what?"

"Never mind, dear. Continue describing the séance."

"Well, uh, Mr. Conan Doyle said he had someone from the Other Side who wanted to talk with his great-grandson. Madame Flora asked who it was. Mr. Conan Doyle said it was Col. Beauregard Hollingsworth Madison, so she asked me to go fetch Father."

Maddy settled into a wingback chair opposite Tilly. Locking eyes with her daughter to keep her attention focused. "And what did the late Colonel say to your father?"

Tilly screwed up her face in thought, trying to remember the exact words. "He said, 'The man I killed with that silver bullet hid a piece of the famous Tristan Quilt here in Caruthers Corners. He brought it with him on the wagon train, transporting it to a cousin in San Francisco. I shot him before he could complete his mission. But he had managed to hide it."

"Tristan Quilt? Are you sure that's what this ghost said?"

"Pretty sure. What's a Tristan Quilt?"

"I'm not sure. Go on with the story."

"Then Dad said, 'How do you know about this?' and Col. Madison said, 'There are no secrets beyond the Pale, laddie. I can help you find this priceless quilt.' And Dad said, 'No, I meant how do you know about the silver bullet?' The Colonel replied, 'Because I fired it into Count Antonio Guicciardini's heart with my very own flintlock in a duel to the death.'"

"Did the spirit say anything else?"

"Just that he had to go, but that Mr. Conan Doyle could find him if we wanted more information about how to find this Tristan Quilt. Isn't that thrilling?"

"Very impressive," Maddy said dryly. What a crock. But that reference to a Tristan Quilt seemed to ring a bell of some sort. She'd have to ask Cookie about it. A friend like Cookie Bentley was like having a living encyclopedia.

~ ~ ~

That very next day Maddy recounted this bizarre tale to the Quilters Club. The ladies met every Tuesday afternoon in the Sewing Room at the Hoople Heritage Quilting Museum. There were four of them in all – Maddy, Cookie, Bootsie, and Lizzie.

Maddy you've now met. Cookie Bentley heads the local Historical Society. Bootsie Purdue runs the no-kill Strays & Rescues Animal Shelter. And Lizzie Ridenour, the best quilter among them, is in charge of the Heritage Quilting Museum where they meet each week.

Two of Maddy's grandchildren sometimes joined them. But Aggie was now enrolled at Yale, and N'yen was wowing them at Northwestern. Aggie's friend Sissy had been a

7

member for a while, but her participation faded after the other two had gone off to college.

"Look, I know this séance business is all fake," Maddy said after telling them the ghost's story. "But how could Madame Flora know so much about Col. Beauregard Madison – the duel, the silver bullet, the quilt?"

"The town's history is easy to find out about," Cookie brushed the mystery away. "Aside from all the displays at the Historical Society, there are several books, the best being *The History of the Indian Territory, 1803 - 1907* by Nelson Lawrence Chadwick. You can find it in any library. And old Jacob Caruthers gave his version in his journal too, although he has been proven to be an unreliable narrator."

"But how did Madame Flora know about the Tristan Quilt?" wondered Lizzie. As director of the Heritage Quilting Museum, she knew a thing or two about rare historical quilts.

"What is this quilt?" asked Maddy. "I think I've heard of it, but I can't place any details."

"The Tristan Quilt is a big deal in quilting history," Lizzie reminded her. "Made around 1360 in Sicily, it is one of the earliest surviving quilts in the world. Only two fragments are known to exist, one on display at the Victoria & Albert Museum in London and the other at the Bargello Palace in Florence."

Cookie drew on her eidetic memory. She was a bit of a freak of nature, with a mind that never forgets. Highly Superior Autobiographical Memory (HSAM) is a condition that has been identified in fewer than 100 people worldwide. "Those two fragments and a sister quilt are the only known surviving medieval quilts. They depict scenes from the story of Tristan and Isolde."

"I don't know that story," said Bootsie. She tended to read paperback romances with bare-chested Fabio's on their covers. Beach reads (without the beach).

"No one's sure of the original author," replied Cookie. "But *Tristan and Isolde* is a 12-Century chivalric romance that recounts the love affair between the Cornish knight Tristan and the Irish princess Isolde. In it, Tristan travels to Ireland to bring back the princess for his uncle, King Mark. Along the way, they ingest a love potion which causes them to fall madly in love. After Isolde marries Tristan's uncle, she and the knight engage in a torrid affair. But the king grows suspicious and seeks to punish them." Her voice sounded rote, as if she were reading from a book.

"Kinda like the love triangle between King Arthur, Genevieve, and Sir Lancelot," observed Maddy. She was known to be a voracious reader. A trait she had passed on to her grandchildren.

"Oh, yeah, I've seen that movie *Camelot*," said Bootsie. "I thought Richard Harris was handsome as King Arthur, but I would've left him in a heartbeat for Franco Nero."

"Apparently Vanessa Redgrave felt the same way," offered Lizzie. The feisty redhead kept up with movie-star gossip. "She had a baby by Franco Nero. And they eventually got married."

"I was referring to Sir Thomas Malory's *Le Morte d'Arthur*," said Maddy. "Although that movie *Camelot* was certainly entertaining."

Cookie shook her head. "While the stories intersect, the Tristan Quilt couldn't have been based on Malory. *Le Morte d'Arthur* was published in 1483. The Quilt was made around 1360 ... or earlier."

"I don't know much about Malory," admitted Maddy. "Just the book."

"Not much is known about Malory. But it's pretty well agreed he was a criminal, a traitor, and a drunkard. He also served time in prison."

Maddy shrugged. "Nonetheless, he did write what's considered the best-ever account of King Arthur and his Round Table."

"He also recounted the adventures of Sir Tristan in Caxton's VIII–XII," Cookie acknowledged. "But he wasn't the first to tell the story."

"So Tristan was a knight in shining armor?" asked Bootsie. Trying to follow the conversation. She ran her fingers through her pixie haircut, an expression of her frustration.

"To Princess Isolde he was," winked Maddy. Trying to suppress a smile. Her tubby friend was easily confused.

"Back to that medieval quilt," Lizzie spoke up, trying to steer the conversation onto the topic that most interested her. She sat there primly at the big work table in the Crafts Room, eyeing her fellow Quilters Clubbers.

"Sorry," said Bootsie. "This is so exciting I've always been fascinated by knights. I read *Ivanhoe* when I was in grade school."

"A good book," Maddy nodded.

"Scottish author Sir Walter Scott published the novel in three parts back in 1819," Cookie drew on her memory.

"Sir Walter Scott?" said Bootsie. "Didn't he found The Lost Colony?"

"You're thinking of Sir Walter Raleigh," smiled Cookie.

Lizzie ignored her friends' ramblings. "Let me get this straight, Maddy. You're saying there's a third previously unknown fragment of the Tristan Quilt somewhere here in Caruthers Corners?"

"Not exactly," Maddy shook her head, making her silver-shaded hair shimmer in the fluorescent light. "I'm saying that's what the supposed manifestation of Col. Beauregard Madison claimed. Which means the information came from Madame Flora. Which makes it questionable."

"You're saying Madam Flora is a fake?" asked Bootsie. Not sure where she stood on the subject of an existence beyond death.

Lizzie gave her a look that she reserved for idiots and unruly children. "Really, Bootsie. Do you think that crazy old charlatan can conjure up the spirit of Maddy's husband's long-dead ancestor?"

Bootsie looked sheepish. "Well, I've always thought the Hoople Mansion might be haunted."

That got a chortle out of Cookie. "I recall you thought the same think about Beasley Manor. But we proved that was just a petty criminal hiding out there in the abandoned building."

"None of the renters at Beasley Arms –" the building had been converted into a low-income apartment building "– have complained about any ghosts," Lizzie pointed out, simply to side against Bootsie. The two had been at odds lately, something to do about a stray dog that got turned in to the shelter. Turned out to be Lizzie's Volpino, a small spitz-like pup named "Michelangelo" (because it's believed that the painter Michelangelo owned one). She'd been snippy ever since.

"Okay, okay," Bootsie threw up her hands. "But I find it hard to believe in the Father, the Son, and the Holy Ghost, then deny that ghosts exist."

"Are you saying Jesus is a ghost?" goaded Lizzie.

"No, Rev. Kilroy says Jesus rose from the dead. That makes him alive. Isn't that what Easter's all about?" Rev. James Noah Kilroy ("Kilroy was here," he ended each sermon) served as minister at Pleasant Meadows, the Baptist church with the tall spire that's located on the backside of the Town Square.

"Who is this Holy Ghost anyway?" asked Lizzie. She was not all that religious when it came down to it. Her Italian forbearers were Catholics, but the closest cathedral was over

11

in Burpyville, so she wasn't what you'd call a "practicing Catholic."

Cookie had something more to add. "For most Christian denominations, the Holy Spirit, or Holy Ghost, is believed to be the third person of the Trinity – a Triune with each entity in fact being God."

"Three-in-one?" said Bootsie.

"Yes," nodded Cookie. Ever since her first husband Bob had died, she'd had a religious bent. She still put flowers on his grave, even after marrying Ben Bentley. Kind of a peace offering.

"Does that mean the Holy Ghost haunts churches?" asked Bootsie, totally confused.

"Don't worry about it too much," advised Maddy. "Even the church leaders can't agree. There's a whole branch of theology called Pneumatology that's devoted to studying the subject."

"Even so, Trinitarianism – the Holy Trinity, that is – was declared to be official Christian doctrine at the First Ecumenical Council in 325 AD," Cookie pointed out. "And in 381 AD the First Council of Constantinople reaffirmed the divinity of the Holy Spirit."

"Well, I guess that makes it official," shrugged Bootsie, considering the argument settled. "Ghosts are real."

"Not exactly –" began Cookie.

"About the Tristan Quilt," Lizzie tried to get back the group back on track. "Are you saying – uh, I mean, is the ghost saying – that a piece of the Tristan Quilt is hidden somewhere here in Caruthers Corners."

"That's what Tilly reported. Aunt Hilda and Aunt Helga were witnesses. Beau, too."

"Who else was at the séance?"

"Just two others – Dorothy Stargazer, the town's new librarian; and Faith Ann Crackleton, who is technically my aunt."

"Faith Ann? My Gus's mother?" exclaimed Cookie. She and her husband Ben were in the process of adopting Gus Crackleton. His mother had far too many unwanted children, fathers unknown.

Maddy nodded. "Yes, I'm afraid so. Aunt Hilda invited her. Faith Ann is actually my biological father's younger sister."

"And Aunt Hilda and Aunt Helga are not actually your aunts," Cookie pointed out. She was the keeper of local genealogy charts, part of her duties at the Historical Society.

She was right: The so-called Hoople Quadruples – Hilda, Helga, Helena, and Herbert – had been a sham, four unrelated orphans passed off as quads. They toured the world making appearances before royalty and stadiums filled with cheering fans, before their "parents" were exposed as pulling off "*Le Grand Rouge*" (as *La Monde* had termed it at the time) or "Deception Times Four" (as a *New York Times* headline put it). In short, a masterful con job.

A few years ago Maddy's father had been revealed to be Herbert Hoople, one of the famous foursome. And DNA tests had proved that Herbie was Faith Ann's abandoned older brother – a Crackleton.

"Biologically speaking, my father was your soon-to-be adopted son's uncle," teased Maddy. "Doesn't that make you my aunt or something like that?"

"Really!" huffed Cookie. "It doesn't work like that."

With all the twisted lineages in Caruthers Corners, it was easy to wind up like that old Lonzo and Oscar ditty, "I'm My Own Grandpaw." The Crackleton Clan was known for its consanguinity – a genetic Petri dish that had produced such freakish conditions as polydactylism, microcephaly, lymphedema, and even an omphalopagus twin.

Maddy was troubled by her mitochondrial connections to these medical oddities. Could these errant genes account for Tilly's growing detour from reality? Unlike Kellyanne Conway's "alternate facts," Matilda Tidemore seemed to have embraced an "alternate reality," a world filled with fairies and spirits and unicorns – having little resemblance to 21st-Centure Indiana.

"Beau was only at the séance for a short while," Maddy continued the story. "They called him into the room when the spirit guide asked for him."

"Spirit guide?"

"A supposed intermediary between Madame Flora and the Other Side. She claims he's the ectoplasmic embodiment of Sir Arthur Conan Doyle."

"Do you mean the man who wrote *The Adventures of Sherlock Holmes*?" responded Lizzie.

"That's what Tilly says."

"Makes a kind of cockeyed sense," nodded Cookie. "Aside from being a popular author, Arthur Conan Doyle was a great believer in spiritualism. He and Harry Houdini broke up their longstanding friendship over the topic. Doyle fervently believed in séances, poltergeists, spirit photography, and the Cottingley Fairies. Houdini didn't."

"Let me get this straight," said Bootsie. "Madam Flora uses a ghost to introduce her to other ghosts?"

"Something like that."

"Where does Beau come in?" asked Cookie.

"When the spirit guide asked to speak to Beauregard Hollingsworth Madison the Fourth, Tilly called him into the room."

"And Beau spoke to the spirit guide, this Arthur Conan Doyle?"

"Yes." Maddy rolled her eyes as she repeated the story. "Beau asked him whether John Watson had been shot in the leg or the shoulder. The Sherlock Holmes books have it both ways."

"Was that a test?"

"No, Beau was just curious. He's a Sherlock Holmes fan."

"What did the spirit guide answer?" asked Lizzie.

"He said both the leg and the shoulder. But Beau didn't buy that. He figured the answer should have been one or the other. He thought the whole thing was a fake – until the spirit guide mentioned the murders."

"What murder?" Now she had Bootsie's complete attention. As it happens, cop's wives have an extraordinary interest in murders.

"Two of them. Count Antonio Guicciardini – the guy who hid a scrap of the Tristan Quilt. And a more recent one, he didn't say whom."

"Guicciardini," nodded Cookie. "That's the name of the Sicilian family associated with the Tristan Quilt. According to the Victoria and Albert Museum, the quilt was a wedding gift to Pietro di Luigi Guicciardini and Laodomia Acciaiuli in 1395 ... although some researchers suggest an earlier date."

"How do you remember this stuff?" asked Lizzie. She could barely remember where to find her car keys.

"Beats me. Facts just stick in my head."

"About that murder –?" Bootsie returned to the question at hand.

"Oh yes," Maddy picked up the story. "The ghost of Col. Beauregard Madison the First told them that he shot this Count Guicciardini with a silver bullet in a duel."

"Why did that get Beau's attention?" asked Cookie, brow knitted with curiosity. "Didn't he know about the duel? That's a historical fact."

"Yes, but nobody knew about the silver bullet. Did you?"

"Uh, well, no."

"The actual silver slug was handed down from Col. Madison to Number Two who handed it down to Number Three who handed it down to my Beau, Number Four. That bullet has been a family secret, no way anyone could have known about it. I didn't even know about it 'til now."

"Holy moly," said Bootsie. "Are you saying Madam Flora and her spirit guide are the real deal? How else would they know this?"

"Beau can't explain it. He's worrying over it."

"What do *you* think?" pressed Lizzie, leaning forward for an answer.

"I don't know where Madame Flora got her information. But it makes me think if she got it right about the silver bullet – and Beau confirms that's true – she might also have it right about the Tristan Quit."

"You're saying a piece of one of the rarest quilts in the world is hidden somewhere here in our little town?" repeated Lizzie, eyebrows raised with incredulity.

"It's possible."

"Come on," frowned Cookie. "That's a bit of a stretch, don't you think? A very rare quilt made in Italy during the Middle Ages finding its way to a small out-of-the-way town in the Midwest – that seems pretty farfetched."

"I suppose it is," shrugged Maddy. "But the ghost of Col. Beauregard Madison – uh, the glowing light on the ceiling – knew about the silver bullet. That gives Madame Flora some credibility."

"So what are you saying?" asked Lizzie.

"That I think the Quilters Club ought to look into it."

Chapter Three

Quilts and Crooks

As you might expect, the members of the Quilters Club spent their spare time stitching patchwork quilts and doing appliqués and making trapunto coverlets. Their handiwork was on display in the retail section of the Hoople Quilting Heritage Museum, a fundraising effort that helped support the museum. Designs ranged from traditional Log Cabin patterns to Nine Patches, Flying Geese quilts to Bear Paws, Drunkard's Paths to Lattice Squares. And the prices were reasonable too.

Over the years the four women who made up this little quilting bee had been drawn into a number of local mysteries – like those Lost Boys who turned up 30 years later, or finding a patchwork quilt stuffed with rare "watermelon dollars," locating a missing statue of a Town Founder, chasing down Viking treasures and runestones, digging up a hidden wagonload of gold, sighting UFOs, taking part in a magic act that brought back the dead, thwarting a mad scientist who tried to poison the town's water supply, catching those thieves who stole Capt. Percival Perricock's antediluvian fossil collection, uncovering false family trees and fake adoption agencies, as well as engaging with scary witches, Potawatomi Indians, Russian spies, and phony historic quilts that needed exposing.

As a result, they had gained quite a reputation as amateur detectives.

The *Burpyville Gazette* once called them "a quartet of Miss Marples." Maddy was flattered. She was a big fan of Agatha Christie puzzlers.

If anyone could figure out the truth behind the Tristan Quilt and that silver bullet, it was Maddy Madison and her Quilters Club friends.

~ ~ ~

Beau was puzzled by his experience at the séance. Everybody had been seated around a round table in the center of the room. The lights were so dim he could barely make out their silhouettes – his daughter Tilly, that medium lady, Aunt Hilda and Aunt Helga, the new librarian, and that Crackleton cuckoo. He'd just stepped into the room when a glow up near the ceiling flickered on and a male voice (British, it sounded like) greeted him by name. That was kinda spooky.

How the spirit knew the story of the silver bullet was beyond him. Nobody in the Madison family ever talked about it. He hadn't even mentioned it to his wife 'til after this encounter with Arthur Conan Doyle ... or whoever the heck it was there in the dark. Madam Flora claimed it was a spirit guide, but he didn't believe that for a New York Minute.

The silver bullet – the actual, real, passed-down-from-father-to-son silver bullet – was locked away in Beau's gun safe. Beau wasn't a gun nut, he didn't even go hunting. And Maddy was for banning everything from slingshots to Uzis. But he owned a Colt M1911, a souvenir from his years in Vietnam. And with grandchildren running all around the Mansion, he thought it proper to keep it locked away.

This government-issued single-action, semi-automatic, magazine-fed, recoil-operated pistol was chambered for a .45 ACP cartridge. The M1911 served as the standard-issue sidearm for the US military from 1911 to 1985, widely used in World War I, World War II, the Korean War, and the Vietnam War. The US procured approximately 2.7 million M1911 and M1911A1 pistols during its service life. Many pistols made their way back to the States in the luggage of returning vets.

Next to the Colt M1911 in the safe was a box of cartridges, Federal .45 ACP 230 grain HST. And next to that was a small box with cotton batting that held a round lump of silver. This was the bullet that killed Count Antonio Guicciardini on June 12, 1832. Beau's great-grandfather had pulled the trigger. But that wasn't part of the family secret. All the history books mentioned the duel.

Maybe the books didn't mention the silver bullet, but that wasn't the important part. The real secret was *why* he pulled the trigger.

Chapter Four

Hands Across the Sea

Aggie was in the parlor of the 52-room Hoople Mansion when she heard a knock at the front door. Swinging the massive oak door open, she came face-to-face with a pretty blonde woman with a suitcase next to her. She looked as ethereal as an angel.

"Who are you?" blurted Aggie, startled by this strange visage.

"I am you," the visitor smiled.

~ ~ ~

"Oh my goodness," said Maddy Madison, her hand pressed to her bosom, as if trying to steady her beating heart. "Come in, come in."

"Sorry to drop in without warning," said the blonde in a merry voice that sounded vaguely like Marybelle Olsen, the British housekeeper who managed the Hoople Mansion. "My husband had an unexpected meeting in Indianapolis. I simply could not be that close to Caruthers Corners and not stop by."

"Oh, I hope you will stay for a while."

"Perhaps a few days, if that is all right."

"Yes, of course. You will always be a part of this family."

The woman glanced around the interior of the Mansion, taking in the parlor and dining room and great room, all within eyesight of the foyer. "The family has increased quite a bit since I was last here," she observed.

Aggie Tidemore squinted toward the visitor. "I know who you are," she said, a moment of revelation crossing her face. "You're the exchange student, Leslie Ann Holmes. I've heard about you all my life."

The pretty blonde smiled at the girl. "It's Lady Greystone now. That because I'm married to Oliver Trent, the Earl of Greystone. But you can call me Leslie Ann."

"Y-you're married to an earl?" stammered Aggie. "Does that make you a countess?"

"It does indeed. But no need to get hung up with titles among friends and family."

Aggie grinned. "I see what you meant about being me. You were the first Aggie. The original junior member of the Quilters Club."

"I prefer to think of you as the second Leslie Ann."

"So you really helped Grammy and Lizzie and Cookie and Bootsie solve crimes?"

"One or two. But I understand you have quite a track record for yourself. Perhaps we can compare notes while I'm here." (Note: See *The Christmas Quilt*, Book 7 in the Quilters Club Mysteries series.)

Maddy spoke up. "Let's get you settled in. Then we can all catch up. Your letters have been great. But there's nothing like a face-to-face confab over a pot of tea."

"What are you doing here?" Leslie Ann asked Aggie. "Your grandmother wrote that you were at school. Yale, right?"

"We're between semesters," said Aggie, chipper as usual. "I came home to help the Quilters Club solve a mystery."

"Hmm, I hear you're pretty good at it," said the blonde visitor. She and Aggie could have passed for sisters, other than the visitor's British accent.

"My cousin N'yen is better than me. He's a certifiable genius. He's coming down from Chicago to join us."

"Your cousin is going to Northwestern, am I correct?"

"Yep, their advanced admission program. He's barely sixteen, two years younger than me."

"Oh my, I barely remember when I was your age."

"You were fifteen when you came here as an exchange student. I'd just been born."

"Yes," smiled the young Brit. "I used to babysit you. You were cranky and colicky, as I recall."

"Well, I'm not longer colicky," Aggie laughed. She liked this newcomer. She seemed like an older sister she'd never had. Aggie had never been close to her younger sisters – the "Trio of Trouble," she called them.

At that moment Marybelle Olsen breezed into the room, almost as if floating on air. "Welcome, my dear," she greeted the visitor. "It's so good to hear a familiar voice. One speaking proper English."

"You must be Marybelle. Maddy says wonderful things about you in her letters."

"You two write letters back and forth?" asked Aggie. Surprised at this antiquated means of communication. "I would have thought you would've simply emailed each other."

Maddy chuckled at her granddaughter's words. "Guess I'm just an old fuddy-duddy," she blushed.

"In England, we're trained to observe all the polite amenities. A written letter is much more personal than an email or a text or a tweet," winked Leslie Ann. She was pretty down to earth for a British countess.

"Guess I can see that," Aggie admitted.

"Perhaps you should give it a try with your cousin N'yen," suggested Mrs. Olsen, a twinkle in her eye.

"That would be a waste of paper," responded Aggie. "That little nerd doesn't know how to read anything that isn't made up of pixels."

Marybelle Olsen nodded toward the visitor. "Follow me, Lady Greystone. I'll take you to your room. You can get settled in and then we'll have tea."

"That would be lovely," smiled the blonde. Then she turned to Maddy and the girl. "Could I ask a favor?"

"Of course, anything."

"If I'm going to be here a few days, could I join the Quilters Club in looking into this mystery Aggie was telling me about?"

Chapter Five

"Quilters Club, Assemble!"

N'yen Madison arrived that next day. He was on his summer break at Northwestern. Maddy kept a suite for him at the Hoople Mansion. In the past few years the young Vietnamese boy had spent as much time here as he had with his parents in Chicago. He loved being with his Grammy and Grampy. He and his cousin Aggie were all but inseparable. And lately he seemed to have a mild crush on Aggie's friend, Cecelia LaToya Jackson.

"Hello," he greeted Leslie Ann. "Are you a real princess?"

"No," she laughed. "But I am a countess."

"Does that make your husband a count – like Count Chocula?"

"Silly, don't you know anything about British royalty," scolded Aggie. "You probably think Burger King is a real king."

"Hey, is that any way to greet your favorite cousin?"

"You're adopted, so you're really not my cousin."

"Better not let Grammy hear you say that. She says family isn't based on bloodlines."

"That's because she was adopted too. You outcasts stick together."

Leslie Ann held up a hand, like a stop signal. "Aggie and N'yen, I know you two are just kidding around. But don't get carried away. I feel as much a member of this family as my family back in London. Bloodlines have nothing to do with it. Agnes knows that."

"Sorry," said Aggie.

"It's really nice to be here," said Leslie Ann. "I feel like you are the sister I never had." She turned to N'yen. "And you're my little brother."

"So you're really a countess?" he said.

She nodded. "My husband is the Earl of Greystone. And according to British peerage that makes me an honest-to-goodness countess. But no need to be formal. You can just call me Leslie Ann. After all, I used to change the diapers on your cousin Agnes."

"Yuk."

"About eighteen years ago I was an exchange student, part of the Hands Across the Sea program. I was lucky enough to live with your grandparents for a year. I loved it here. And I loved being a part of the Madison family."

N'yen cocked his head. "And you're back for a visit?"

"Yes, my husband had a meeting in Indianapolis, and being so close I thought I'd drop by to see my old family and friends. Your grandmother and I have kept in close touch over the years."

"I've heard about you," said N'yen. "You were one of the first members of the Quilters Club. Grammy says you were a pretty good detective."

"I wasn't bad, if I do say so myself." She pretended to dust off her lapel, a parody of braggadocio.

"Are you going to help us with this new case – the one with a ghost?"

"If you'll have me. But I must warn you that I do not believe in ghosts."

"Then you and I are on the same page," the boy grinned. "We have to find out how that medium lady found out about Grampy's silver bullet."

"N'yen Madison," said his cousin Aggie, her hands firmly on her hips, a scowl crossing her heart-shaped face. "Has Northwestern University replaced your brain with one marked Abby Normal? Our sleuthing has nothing to do with that stupid Lone Ranger silver bullet. Our task is to find that missing fragment of that medieval quilt."

~ ~ ~

Maddy was saying the same thing to the Quilters Club the next day. They had met at the Heritage Quilting Museum to launch their investigation. Although scavenger hunt might have been a better description. "Where would you hide a quilt if your wagon train had just been stalled hereabout?"

"Why hide it in the first place?" asked Cookie.

"Maybe someone was following you, trying to steal it," suggested Bootsie. Trying to think like her husband, Police Chief Jim Purdue. He always suspected larceny in others.

"Ooo, this sounds like a juicy spy story," said Lizzie. "A mysterious count smuggling a valuable cargo across country, aware that he's being tracked by nefarious foreign agents."

"So where would he hide it?" repeated Maddy.

"Put it inside a watertight jug and lower it down a well."

"Hide it in a cave."

"Stick it inside a hollow tree trunk."

"Place it in the cornerstone of a building."

"Bury it."

There were plenty of ideas, but none sounded right. The biggest concern – if the story were true – was that the scrap of fabric had been well enough protected that it would not have rotted away or been consumed by mildew after nearly two centuries in the ground.

~ ~ ~

The buzzer announced someone entering the Quilting Heritage Museum. Lizzie popped up from her chair to greet the museum's visitors. The rare Renaissance Quilt on permanent display in the gallery pulled in quite a few curiosity-seekers.

Maddy and the others waited in the crafts room. They had been working on their latest quilts as they talked about how to find the Tristan Quilt. Everybody was doing a Crazy Quilt for an upcoming Silent Auction – a fundraiser.

"Look who's here," announced Lizzie as she ushered in the trio. "Aggie, N'yen, and Leslie Ann – uh, that is Lady Greystone."

"I'm still Leslie Ann," the blonde woman smiled modestly. "A fancy title doesn't change me from being the same person as the exchange student who helped you solve that mystery of the Thomas Nast Christmas quilt eighteen years ago."

"What are you girls doing here?" asked Maddy. "I thought you three were going to check out that new exhibit at the museum." The Perricock Museum of Science & History, that megalith that occupies the hill adjacent to the Hoople Mansion, had an exhibit about trilobites, those fossilized cockroach-like creatures (a type of marine arthropod) that lived during the Paleozoic Era.

"The trilobite exhibit will be up for three months," said Aggie. "Plenty of time to see it."

"And I'm only here for a few days," enjoined Leslie Ann. "That doesn't leave us much time to find that lost Tristan Quilt."

"You're going to help?" blurted Bootsie, surprised by this turn of events. Being of a more common background, she had a more elevated conception of British royalty.

"Think of us as reinforcements," said Leslie Ann. "The more brains on the case the better."

"Yes," added N'yen. "Like linking computers into a network to get more power."

"Excellent," said Cookie. "Let's get started."

Chapter Six

The Confidence Game

Florence Eleanor Bashinski – Madam Flora, that is – had a husband. Or maybe he was an ex-husband. They had been married and divorced seven times, to the point that the pair had lost count whether they were currently wed or not.

Heinrich Bashinski was a small man, barely 5 feet, with a thin moustache, bug eyes, and no hair. He had a long record as a con man, his favorite scam being the Wallet Drop, although in recent times he was having a fair amount of success with the Melon Drop variation and the Classic Pengci. Sometimes he and his wife also pulled the Bogus Dry Cleaning Bill Scam or the Wedding Planner Scam, but lately Bujo cons were working well.

Bujo is a Romani word for "bag," that being the way money is usually delivered in this Fortune Telling confidence game. Here, a fortune teller uses cold reading skills to detect a client who is genuinely troubled rather than one merely seeking entertainment. Often, it's a gambler complaining of bad luck. Or someone who has lost his job. Or someone who has just lost out in the game of love. The fortune teller informs the mark that they are the victim of a curse, and that for a fee a spell can be cast to remove the curse. The victim brings money in a bag to have a magic incantation said over it, and leaves with a bag of worthless paper. Florence was adept at pulling a smooth switcheroo.

You can only pull these scams so long before the police get wind of you. That's why the duo had left Indianapolis and were working their way through small upstate towns. Today,

Florence was passing herself off as Madame Flora; last month it had been Mystic Francessa; and before that, Sofia of Safed.

Their latest pigeon was this woman named Matilda Tidemore, a rich kook married to a local mayor. The Tidemores lived in a big castle overlooking Caruthers Corners, a town up near the Ohio State line. Tilly, as she called herself, had bought into Madame Flora's spiel – hook, line, and sinker – even roping in her two moneybags aunts and a couple of others. This promised to be a big haul.

This time the scam required the mark to put up money to help locate a priceless objet d'art, a missing quilt. This was akin to a Nigerian Scam, an advance-fee fraud. One of the most common types of confidence games, it typically involves promising the victim a large sum of money in return for a small up-front payment.

Heinrich was brilliant at coming up with these scams. He had a knack for this kind of thing. It only took a little research – a visit to the town's history museum, a few cups of coffee listening to gossip at a local diner, some digging in the back issues of the *Burpyville Gazette* – to identify the target and come up with a fanciful "pot at the end of the rainbow," in this case a rare quilt.

Yeah, they were going for a long con here.

A "long con" or "big con" is a flimflam that unfolds over several days or weeks; it often involves props, sets, and costumes. It aims to rob the victim of huge sums of money, often by convincing them to empty out bank accounts and borrow from family members. The Hoople-Madison-Tidemore family should be good for millions.

~ ~ ~

Samuel Thompson (1821–1856) inspired the term "confidence man." He was a swindler who asked his victims to show their confidence in him by giving him money or letting him hold their watch. Thompson was arrested in July 1849.

A reporter with *The New York Herald* referred to Thompson as "The Confidence Man" in his story. The term got shortened in popular parlance to "con man."

A few weeks later, *National Police Gazette* coined the term "confidence game" to describe this profession of the criminally minded.

~ ~ ~

Madame Flora wasn't eager for this con to end. After all, she had it good. She was ensconced in a luxurious bedroom in the Tidemore family's wing of the Hoople Mansion. The bed was comfy, the food was delicious, and the mark and her dotty old aunts treated her like she was their ticket to Heaven.

Her husband was staying in a cheap room at the Highliner Hotel in Burpyville, the next town over. His accommodations were not so comfortable. He complained about springs in the bed poking him, the peeling wallpaper, and a dripping sink in the bathroom. Room service consisted mainly of greasy grilled cheese sandwiches or burgers that tasted like cardboard. He was more than ready to complete this scam and move on. Chicago would be their next stop. That was a real city with real hotels and real beds.

So far, they had completed the first three stages of a confidence game: (1) The Foundation Work, (2) the Approach, and (3) the Build-Up.

Next would come: (4) the Convincer, (5) the Hurrah, and (6) the In-and-In. However, this con might require another stage, (7) the Corroboration. Some games, particularly those involving something fake, require an accomplice to play the part of an uninvolved third party who confirms the claims made by the con man (or woman, in this case).

Heinrich didn't have to come in until that last stage, when he would play the dual role of corroborator and the interested bystander who puts money into the scheme along with the victim to create the appearance of legitimacy.

Their last haul was $25,000. But with the Hoople Quadruplet Trust Fund, this one could amount to millions. This could be the Big One, the capstone of what had been up till now a penny-ante career in crime.

That's why Heinrich and Florence had picked the Tristan Quilt as their bait. This medieval bedcovering was worth zillions. And Tilly Tidemore's mother, being part of a serious quilting bee, would recognize the quilt's value.

It was lucky he'd bought that old journal from a rare manuscript dealer down in Indy. And the letter. That's what gave him the idea about the quilt.

Too bad the guy had to die.

Chapter Seven

The Silver Bullet

Beau Madison was puzzled that his great-grandfather – or a trickster pretending to be the ghost of his ancestor – had known about the silver bullet. All that gobbledygook about the hidden fragment of a rare Italian quilt aside, that lump of silver was the key to a family secret.

Part of the secrecy was because that bullet was proof that Col. Beauregard Hollingsworth Madison actually had killed someone after the duel was over. Not that Col. Madison had any penalty to face, having been dead himself 137 years now. But the stigma of a cold-blooded murder would hang over the descendants of the Town Founder like a shroud.

The second reason for the silence was that none of his progeny wanted the old man's legacy sullied by accusations of lunacy. Nobody would believe the story. Who would accept the fact that his great-grandfather had shot a werewolf?

~ ~ ~

This dark corner of the Madison Family History had never been written down, no diary, no notes, just an oral tradition passed from father to son.

Beau had yet to complete the link, to pass the story on to his son. He'd have to do that soon ... now that the proverbial cat was out of the bag. How had that phony fortune teller glommed onto that piece of arcanc information?

Problem was, which son to enlighten? Generally, the info was passed to the eldest son, but his boy Bill was not the type to buy into superstition and tall tales. Bill and Kathy ran a non-profit children's center in Chicago. They barely had time for their own youngster, N'yen. Bill didn't care about Caruthers Corners or its Founders

His son Freddie was a more likely candidate to accept the werewolf story. He and Amanda were great parents to little Donna Ann. Maybe coming so close to dying in that Atlanta fire had given Freddie a greater appreciation for life. And a broader imagination than his brother Bill.

Beau's daughter Tilly was youngest of the three. A tad "fragile," she was certainly the type to believe in werewolves and witches. But the established practice was to entrust the family history to a son. Sexist, yes. But tradition was tradition – like that *Fiddler on the Roof* song said.

Tilly's husband Mark didn't count, did he? He was a son-in-law, not a blood relative. But did that matter? N'yen wasn't either, being adopted. And Donna Ann was adopted too. So did genetics really matter?

Strange thoughts for the descendant of a Town Founder.

The more he thought about it, the more he realized it had to be Bill. He was the only one with a male heir to pass the story along to. And that was the tradition, wasn't it?

~ ~ ~

In folklore, a bullet cast from silver is a weapon that will kill a werewolf or vampire. A silver bullet has 10% less density than lead and gives better penetration due to its higher shear modulus. A silver bullet is slightly slower than lead bullets and therefore tends to be less accurate. But at three feet, it's hard to miss.

Some say the idea that a silver bullet kills werewolves can be traced back to a real event: In 1640, the city of Greifswald, Germany, was said to be infested by werewolves. Legends maintained that shapeshifters were vulnerable to silver, so "a clever lad suggested that they gather all their silver buttons, goblets, belt buckles, and so forth, and melt them down into bullets for their flintlocks and pistols ... this time they slaughtered the creatures and rid Greifswald of the lycanthropes."

Another story told of south-central France being terrorized in 1767 by a man-eating animal known as the Beast of Gévaudana. This wolf-like creature was eventually killed by a hunter who melted down silver medals of the Virgin Mary to make bullets.

In the 19th Century, the Brothers Grimm collected a story called "The Two Brothers" (Tale Number 60) in which the twin brother of a king who'd been killed by a witch shot the old woman dead using three silver buttons from his tunic.

A 1941 horror film – *The Wolf Man* starring Lon Chaney Jr. – was the first cinematic suggestion that werewolves were vulnerable to silver objects, such as a silver-tipped cane, a blade, or a bullet.

Beau recalled seeing *The Wolf Man* on a double feature with *Frankenstein Meets the Wolf Man* at Hinkle's Drive-In. He remembered an incantation that villagers chanted in that film:

> *"Even a man who is pure in heart, and says his*
> *prayers by night;*
> *May become a wolf when the wolfbane blooms*
> *and the autumn moon is bright."*

He thought that was silly, the idea that wolfbane – a flowering plant belonging to the *Ranunculaceae* family – could transform a man into a monster. A known poison, it was more likely to kill someone than turn him into a snarling werewolf.

But how did that explain the werewolf that Col. Beauregard Madison had shot?

Chapter Eight

Sissy's Return

A confidence man exploits human vulnerabilities such as dishonesty, greed, and gullibility. The Quilters Club could not be accused of dishonesty or greed, but they were certainly gullible when it came to hopes of discovering a missing fragment of a historic quilt.

Cookie Bentley called on her photographic memory, quoting from a blurb by the Textile Research Center:

> "The Sicilian Tristan Quilt, also known as the Tristan and Isolde Quilt, or the Guicciardini Quilt, is perhaps the oldest extant European quilt. It dates to the late fourteenth century, and was made in Sicily. It shows scenes from the story of Tristan and Isolde."

"We know all that," groaned Lizzie.

Cookie continued doggedly, "The Victoria and Albert Museum acquired their piece of the quilt in 1904. The Bargello got theirs in 1927. The quilt originally belonged to the Guicciardini family of Sicily, a wedding gift. The Bargello acquired their quilt directly from Count Paolo Guicciardini."

"Another count," said Bootsie.

"European counts are not all that rare," laughed Leslie Ann. "My husband is one."

"I thought he was an earl," said the police chief's wife. Confused as usual.

"A count is a foreign word for an earl, and both their wives are called countess," Leslie Ann explained. "Technically, an earl's wife does not gain the title of countess by marriage, but it's kind of honorary."

"When will we get to meet your earl?" asked Cookie. Returning to the real world as if shaking off a trance-like stupor. Polite amenities providing a touchstone to normalcy.

"In a couple of days, when he comes to pick me up for our flight back to London. I'm sure you will like him. He certainly swept me off my feet."

"How long have you been married?" asked Lizzie, always looking for gossip. "Maddy never tells us anything."

"Leslie Ann got married about four years ago, when I was in the hospital for that small stroke," interjected Maddy. "That's why Beau and I couldn't attend the wedding."

Leslie Ann added, "And the wedding was why I couldn't fly over here to be at Maddy's bedside. She's always been like a second mother to me."

"Back to the quilt," said N'yen, bored by all this talk of marriage. As a 16-year-old, he had little interest in the subject.

Aggie agreed. She and Bobby Elwood had been on a forced break, since she went off to college. Marriage held little interest. "Is it true that my great-great-great grandfather shot this Count Guicciardini to get the quilt?"

"No, no," chuckled Maddy. "It had nothing to do with the quilt. Col. Madison shot the count over an entirely different matter. Beau won't say what it was. Apparently, the count had already hidden his piece of the Tristan Quilt before the duel took place."

"A duel? Like an Old West gunfight?" said N'yen.

"More like the duel between Alexander Hamilton and Aaron Burr than the opening scene on that old TV show *Gunsmoke*," corrected Cookie.

"Oh yeah, where Marshal Matt Dillon draws his six-shooter against a bad guy."

"That's right. But Col. Madison was involved in a duel, not a shoot-out."

"What's the difference?"

"Western gunfights were a crude form of the 'Southern code duello,' a highly formalized means of solving disputes between gentlemen with swords or pistols that had its origins in European chivalry," explained Cookie. Always the historian. "The main difference is that Western gunfights were based on being a fast draw, the ability to quickly draw a handgun and accurately fire it upon a target in the process."

"Quick Draw McGraw," Aggie chimed in. It was one of her favorite TV cartoons. All her classmates at Yale watched cartoons on Saturday mornings if they didn't have classes.

"I'd say it's more like the Gunfight at the O.K. Corral," responded N'yen. He didn't have much use for television cartoons.

"A duel is much more orderly than a gunfight," explained Cookie. "It's an arranged engagement between two people with matched weapons in accordance with agreed-upon rules."

"Way cool," said N'yen, fascinated by the subject.

"In any case, what we're looking into has nothing to do with that long-ago duel," his grandmother brought them back to reality.

"So we're not trying to solve an old murder?"

"Sorry, dear," Lizzie patted his cheek. "We're looking for a missing quilt."

"But I want to know about that silver bullet that the ghost mentioned," grumbled the Vietnamese boy. "Was Col. Madison a peacekeeper like The Lone Ranger? Is that why he used a silver bullet?"

"Not exactly," said his grandmother. "Col. Beauregard Hollingsworth Madison was a veteran of the War of 1812. That was a conflict between the US and the United Kingdom in support of North American Indians trying to resist westward expansion." She could recite it by heart. You didn't live with the descendent of a Town Founder for 40 years and not learn the story.

"The British and the Indians were on the same side?" asked Aggie, trying to follow the history lesson. She hadn't paid much attention to that class in high school.

Leslie Ann spoke up. "Yes, my ancestors were sided with the Red Indians in that one. But the conflict had more to do with economics, British ships blocking trade in French and allied ports during the Napoleonic Wars."

"Who won?"

"We British beat Napoleon at Waterloo in the Napoleonic Wars. But the War of 1812 was inconclusive, a military draw after two years, seven months, four weeks, and one day," responded the countess.

"Excellent!" applauded Cookie. "*You* certainly paid attention in history class."

"Yes, but as you can imagine, we Brits put a slightly different slant on it. We've never quite got over the American Revolution."

"That's when America got its independence," nodded Aggie.

"Like King George sings in that Broadway play *Hamilton*, 'You'll be back,'" teased Leslie Ann.

"Don't think so," smiled Aggie. "I don't want to speak funny like you."

Leslie Ann laughed. "Did it ever occur that you sound funny to me?"

"You both sound funny to me," sniffed N'yen, who had grown up speaking Vietnamese, a branch of the Mon-Khmer language family. Vietnamese has been described as sounding like birdsong because of its expressive flourishes and the way it seems to flutter along "like the wings of a hummingbird."

"You win ," bowed Leslie Ann. "I've read that Vietnamese is the eighth most difficult language in the world to learn."

"I've spoken it since I was a baby," said N'yen, dusting his lapel to show it was no big deal.

"You should try speaking Cockney," she laughed. "That's a British dialect that uses Rhyming Slang. It's like a different language."

"Is that what you speak?" asked Aggie.

"No, I speak Posh English."

"What's that?"

"Technically my accent is known as 'Upper Received Pronunciation' and is widely associated with the English aristocracy and educational institutions such as Eton and Oxford."

"Fancy," said Aggie.

"You can say that again," nodded N'yen. "But I like it."

~ ~ ~

"The missing quilt," Maddy got the conversation back on track. "Where would Count Guicciardini have hidden it?"

"Where did he live?" asked Bootsie. "Maybe he hid it there."

Cookie closed her eyes for a second, as if she was searching her memory banks. "Hmm, there are not many records on one Antonio Guicciardini," she said. "We have the passenger list on the wagon train. There are no deeds in his name. Tax records don't go back that far. The early census reports just counted heads; didn't list names. There's a death record dated December 19, 1831. Lists death due to 'gunshot.' That's all I've ever seen."

"But there could be more?" asked Aggie.

Cookie nodded. "I remember everything I've ever seen. But, yes, there could be records that I've not seen."

"The Count wasn't here very long," observed Maddy. "Arrived in 1829, died in 1831. Two years."

"Shot by your hubby's great-grandfather, according to the ghost," declared Bootsie, like Perry Mason making an accusation in the courtroom.

"That's not news. The duel was reported in Jacob Caruthers' journal," said Cookie. Sticking to the historical facts.

"But the ghost said –"

"Since when do we believe in ghosts?" asked Aggie. "Didn't we prove that the Ghost of Beasley Manor was just a dumb crook hiding out there in the abandoned building?"

"I believe in ghosts," announced a voice at the door to the crafts room. It was none other than Cecelia LaToya Jackson, Aggie's BFF and N'yen's first crush. Engaged in the conversation about gunfights and duels, nobody had heard the door buzz as she came in.

"You *would* believe in ghosts," laughed Aggie, delighted to see her younger friend. Sissy Jackson had just turned 16, N'yen's age. She had faded away recently, with her two pals being off to college.

"Well, young lady, it's about time you showed up," said Lizzie. "You're getting behind in your quiltmaking. With Aggie off at school, you're my new protégé."

"Me?"

"Who else? You have to start attending the Quilters Club meetings again. We still gather here every Tuesday afternoon."

"Yessum, I will be here after school on Tuesdays from now on. Cross my heart."

"So what drew the Alabama possum out of her hole?" teased Aggie. Delighted to see her friend.

"I heard you two was back in town." She glanced shyly at N'yen. It was obvious she had a crush on him too.

"Want to join us in solving a mystery?" interjected Leslie Ann.

"Who are you?"

"I was you before you were a member of the Quilters Club," she repeated her cryptic mantra.

"Oh, I've heard about you," Sissy snapped her fingers. "That BBC-TV voice was the giveaway. You're the exchange student who stayed with the Madisons one year."

"Righty-O. Before you were born, if I have your age correct. I was here the same year Agnes was born."

"What are you doing here now?"

"Just a quick visit. That's why we have to move fast to solve this puzzle."

"What kinda puzzle?"

So they told her.

Chapter Nine

The Sunday Painters

A couple of years ago, Beau Madison had taken up painting. Mostly he copied the various Hoosier School oils scattered throughout the Mansion. The original Mrs. Hoople had amassed quite a collection.

That inspired Aunt Hilda and Aunt Helga to try their hand too. The pseudo-sisters signed up for an art class at the Hoosier State Senior Recreational Center. Neither showed much promise, but they enjoyed the field trips to sketch local landscapes.

Helga had done some sketching before, back when she had lived a reclusive existence in a little cabin out near the Bottomless Sinkhole, letting people think she was dead. In hiding for years. But that's another story.

Mostly Helga did pencils and charcoals of the neighboring flora and fauna. She wasn't very good at it, but it gave her something to do when she wasn't stitching quilts.

Her sister Hilda had a steadier hand, but lacked style. Her drawings were 4th grade level. Nothing to get excited about.

The once-a-week trips sponsored by the Senior Rec Center were a good outing for the elderly women. The fresh air was good for them. It gave them something to do on Sunday afternoons.

One field trip took them out to Gruesome Gorge State Park, a natural canyon that had once been the settlement of peaceful Potawatomi Indians, an indigenous tribe that had spread across Michigan, Wisconsin, and northern Indiana. Major Samuel Elmsford Beasley had led the shameful 1831 Massacre on this local settlement, slaughtering every man, woman, and child who came within the sights of his men's rifles. Now, tourists wandered the grounds admiring the scenery.

Helga was a bit nervous to go there, because the park's geyser was the supposed scene of her death back in 1982. It was nice to be "back from the dead," as she jokingly called it. The pressure of being a world-famous Hoople Quadruplet was much less now, years after they had been discredited as fakes. The scam hadn't been the four kids' doing – in fact, adopted as babies, they didn't even know that they weren't actually siblings while growing up. Today, Hilda and Helga were psychologically as much sisters as any biological pair might be.

Helga spotted it first. "I think I saw a wolf up there on the canyon rim," she said, nudging her sister who had nearly fallen asleep while sketching a Bradford pear tree. Although favored by landscapers for its beautiful white blooms and stately appearance, the plant was one of the most invasive in the state.

"W-what?"

"A wolf. I just saw one."

"There are no wolves left in Indiana."

"Are too. I saw one also when I lived in my hideaway up near Injun Woods."

"Did not."

"Did too. I made a sketch of it. I've still got that sketchbook somewhere."

"I won't believe it 'til I see it – either in real life or in that sketch you claim to have done."

"Claim? I'll dig out that old drawing and show it to you."

Hilda sniffed. "Wolves haven't been seen in Indiana in a hundred years. The settlers wiped them out just like they did the Indians."

"There have been occasional sightings. "

"Domestic dog and wolf hybrids sometimes escape or run loose and get confused with being a wild wolf."

"What I just saw up there on the ridge wasn't no dog."

"Probably a coyote."

"I know a timber wolf when I see one."

"You know what it could have been? A werewolf."

"A what?"

"I've been thinking about that séance, that message from Col. Madison. Why would he shoot that Italian Count with a silver bullet if the man hadn't been a werewolf or a vampire."

"Like Count Dracula?"

"Or a wolf-man. I'm just saying."

"Aw, go on. You've been imbibing the sherry too much. I will have to ask Marybelle to cut you off."

"What if there are more werewolves hiding here among us? Something killed one of the cows at Old MacDonald's Dairy a month or two ago."

"I heard that it was a Sasquatch that did it. There are them big ape-monsters living out in Never Ending Swamp, I'm told."

"You and your Bigfoot stories. It was a wolf I just saw up there on the rim, not a giant ape."

~ ~ ~

Beau was aggravated that the Hoople sisters insisted on sharing his painting studio. There were over 50 rooms in the big rambling Mansion. You'd think he could have one to himself.

But to Aunt Hilda and Aunt Helga, painting was a social activity rather than an artistic pursuit. That's why they had signed up for that class at the Senior Recreational Center in the first place, a weekly occasion to mingle with other elderly ladies and swap gossip and memories and chitchat. Many of them didn't have close families like Hilda and Helga did – even if the Hoople family was largely "adopted."

Preferring to paint in silence – a time for contemplation and philosophical reverie – Beau found it distracting to have two old ladies yacking while he dabbed oil paint onto a stretched canvas. He tried to plan his painting sessions for times when the Hooples weren't there. Fortunately, Marybelle Olsen posted a schedule for everyone in the family on a bulletin board displayed in the Mansion's massive kitchen.

The housekeeper didn't bother trying to keep up with the schedules for Aggie and N'yen, teenagers being so unpredictable and irregular in their comings and goings. But she kept up with most of the others in the household – the Hoople sisters in particular.

"Oh, there you are!" exclaimed Aunt Hilda on finding Beau in the painting studio. "We were looking for you."

"Oh?"

"Yes," said Aunt Helga. "We had a question about the jasper your great-grandfather shot."

"Count Guicciardini – what about him?" responded Beau cautiously. "Don't know much. I'd never even heard his name before that séance. But Maddy tells me Lizzie and Cookie have traced down his ancestors. A family of bigwigs over in Sicily."

"Sicily – where's that?" inquired Hilda.

"That's an island off the toe of Italy," Beau explained the geography. "There in the Mediterranean Sea."

"You know," Aunt Helga nudged her sister. "That's where all those Mafia types come from. Barney Solitairé's kinfolk came from there."

"Barney – our old maid's son?"

"Right, the one we put through college. Now he manages all our money."

"Oh, that Barney. Is he still working for those mobsters?"

"No, sister dear. He now works for us."

"Yes, I remember. A good boy, that Barney."

It was clear to Beau that the old ladies were getting a bit senile. Next thing you know, they would have to be placed in the Memory Care Ward at Wabash Acres. But for now it came across as bickering. Some people found it cute or endearing. He just found it irritating. But, truth was, they were the ones who invited Maddy and her family into the Hoople Mansion – allowing her to partake of her inheritance in advance, as they put it. So complaining was not an option.

Nevertheless, Beau tried to hurry the sisters along. "What did you want to know about that guy Col. Madison shot, that Count Guicciardini?"

Aunt Hilda had no filters. She blurted, "Why did Col. Madison shoot him? Was he a werewolf?"

"W-what makes you ask that?"

"The silver bullet," said Aunt Helga. "Indiana's known for its werewolves – or as the early French settlers called them, *loup-garou*."

"That's right," nodded Hilda. "Werewolf stories date back to the first French trappers who settled over in Vincennes." Established in 1722 as a French trading post, Vincennes's considered the oldest settlement west of the Appalachians. What's more, it was the first capital of Indiana Territory.

The old ladies rattled on. "Many years ago, even before I was born, it was reported that a wild animal was running loose out near the old French cemetery in Vincennes. People said there were 'queer animals that were not animals at all but people that had been bewitched' in the vicinity. A fellow named John Vachet claimed he was attacked by such a creature and had quite a tussle. He barely escaped with his life."

"And there's another story," added her sister. "A man named Charles Vatchet lived down where the present hospital is located in Vincennes. One night as Mr. Vatchet was going home, a wild animal sprang at him. In the struggle he cut it with his knife and – lo and behold – the creature turned into a man. He gave Mr. Vatchet his name and address and begged that he not tell anyone for one year and a day or he would turn back into an animal. You see, when a werewolf is injured to the extent that it brings blood, the charm is broken."

Beau frowned. "John Vachet, Charles Vatchet – are you sure this isn't the same story?"

"What if it is?" retorted Aunt Hilda. "Just goes to show that it's true. Werewolves have been roaming Indiana for years. Bet your Count was one of them hairy critters."

Beau found it hard to refute their accusation. After all, that was what his great-grandfather had thought. Why else would the Colonel stuff his wedding ring in his old muzzleloader to make a silver bullet?

Chapter Ten

The Werewolf

A werewolf is said to be a human with the ability to shapeshift into a frightening therianthropic hybrid wolf-like creature.

Tales of men changing into wolves go back to ancient times. Greek literature and mythology contained such stories. Herodotus wrote about the Neuri, a tribe who transformed into wolves once every year, and then changed back to their human shape after a few days of rampaging.

Medieval laws in Europe recognized the existence of werewolves, aiming to ensure that "… the madly audacious werewolf do not too widely devastate, nor bite too many of the spiritual flock."

Examples of werewolves roaming the British Isles can be found in the works of the 9th-Century Welsh monk Nennius. He is credited with having written the *Historia Brittonum*, which describes the settlement of Britain and adds to the Arthurian legend.

Pagan traditions associated with wolf-men also persisted in the Scandinavian Viking Age. The Úlfhednar were fighters similar to the Berserkers, who dressed in wolf hides and were reputed to channel the spirits of these animals to enhance their effectiveness in battle.

There were numerous reports of werewolf attacks in 16th-Century France. A number of treatises on werewolves were written during 1595 and 1615. The French used the term "Gerulfi" to describe the creatures.

In England they were called "Warwoolfes."

They took different animal names in other parts of the world. "Werehyenas" in Africa, "Werepumas" in South America," and "Weretigers" in India. In Asian cultures they were sometimes called "Wereleopards."

Over in the New World the Navajo feared witches in wolf's clothing called "Mai-cob." In Canada, stretching down to the Michigan peninsula and upstate New York, these shapeshifters were called the "Loup-garou." In Haiti, "Jé-rouges" tricked mothers into giving away their children by waking them up in the middle of the night when they're disoriented.

In Italy, it was said that a man could turn into a werewolf if he slept outside on a summer night with the full moon shining directly on his face. Hmm, was that what happened to Count Antonio Guicciardini? Beau wondered. After all, the Count was Italian.

~ ~ ~

Being practical minded, Maddy would have laughed at all this werewolf talk. That's why Beau didn't bother mentioning this aspect of the stories handed down through the generations. Fortunately, the Quilters Club was too focused on this missing quilt to worry about silly things like werewolves.

For that matter, he doubted that this stupid quilt even existed. None of his forebears had ever talked about a quilt in their hand-me-down story about killing a shapeshifting wolf-man.

So far, only Maddy's dingbat aunts had figured it out. Now they were on a crusade to identify the *loups-garou* living among them. How nutty could you get?

These days Caruthers Corners had a population of 2,912 (give or take). Everyone knew everybody else. The idea that a werewolf could be hiding among them was ridiculous.

Not to mention that a shapeshifting man-wolf was a ridiculous idea in itself. That would be scientifically impossible, physically changing from human into a wolf.

But the story was what the story was.

Maddy hadn't yet put two and two together to grasp the significance of Col. Madison using a silver bullet to shoot someone. She was usually quicker than that. But she was distracted by the visit of Leslie Ann Holmes – uh, Lady Greystone, that is – and their search for some fabled quilt that had been mentioned by a so-called ghost conjured up by that fake medium.

~ ~ ~

Aunt Hilda and Aunt Helga cornered the three youngsters (if at 18 Aggie still qualified as one) in the game room. They were playing pinball on a rehabbed machine that pictured Spider-Man on the glass backbox. N'yen was ahead by 10,412 points.

"Children," said Aunt Hilda, "could we speak with you for a minute?"

"Sure," said Aggie, trying to be accommodating to the elderly ladies. She and Sissy had been playing darts while waiting their turn at the pinball machine. The room also featured a billiard table, a Ping Pong table, a chess table, various board games, a card table, a TV set hooked up to a Nintendo, and a small circular trampoline.

"Aw, I'm on a winning streak," N'yen complained. Stepping back from the clanging pinball machine.

"You want to speak to me too?" asked Sissy. Always careful not to overstep with white folks. Especially those from past generations when civil rights hadn't been seen as a sign of social progress. Her grandfather said things were backsliding and that people called "deplorables" were crawling out from under rocks. She knew these two old women were kind hearted, but "one must always err on the side of caution," her grandfather told her.

"Yes, dear. Everybody."

"What is it?" asked Aggie. The Hoople sisters looked agitated, as if someone had stolen their crystal decanter of sherry or something.

"You've heard talk about the recent séance, I assume," said Aunt Hilda. She leaned forward like someone imparting a secret.

Aggie nodded politely. "Yes, that's been the talk at the Quilters Club. We're going to find that missing quilt."

"Forget the quilt," said Aunt Helga. "It's that silver bullet we want to warn you about."

"Warn us?" said N'yen.

"Do you know what one uses a silver bullet for?" asked Aunt Hilda.

"To show that you're the Lone Ranger." N'yen was being a smart aleck. He was that age.

"No, no, no. It's what you use to kill a werewolf."

"A what?" laughed Aggie.

"Did you say 'werewolf'?" exclaimed Sissy, hurriedly making the sign of a cross over her chest. Even though she'd been raised as a Southern Baptist, she knew the proper symbols to ward off ghosts and demons and werewolves.

"You two are just trying to scare us," accused N'yen. "Like telling spooky stories before bedtime."

"No, we just want you children to be safe," said Hilda. "We think there are wolf-men on the loose. The town is crawling with them."

"That's why we want to give you this," said her sister. "Sleep with it in bed. Werewolves hate silver."

The two elderly women passed out their "gifts" – a silver platter to N'yen, a silver serving dish to Sissy, and a silver candlestick to Aggie.

"Are you serious?' asked N'yen, looking down at his reflection in the shiny platter.

"Those items are pure silver," Hilda assured them.

"That's right – three nines fine, not sterling," nodded Helga.

"Werewolves?" repeated Aggie. What a crazy idea. These old loons had completely lost their marbles, she told herself.

"Thank you," said Sissy. "I'm gonna sleep with this dish under my goose-down pillow to keep away werewolves, vampires, and other boogers."

N'yen just rolled his eyes with disbelief. This reminded him of when the nutty old women had seen a Gollywompus in the backyard three or four months ago. It turned out to be a vagrant named Possum Johnson.

"Don't tell your grandfather that we told you about the werewolf," whispered Hilda.

"That's right," nodded Helga. "He says it's a family secret."

Chapter Eleven

Dinnertime Deliria

At dinner, the talk was all about that missing scrap of quilt. Marybelle had orchestrated a traditional British repast – steak and kidney pudding with mashed potatoes and green peas.

Leslie Ann was delighted. "I haven't had any true 'home cooking' in weeks," she complimented the housekeeper. "This is delicious."

"Not bad," admitted Beau, cautiously cutting into the suet-crust pastry to taste the diced beef and kidney in a pool of onion-flavored gravy.

"This guacamole salad is good too," said Tilly. The kitchen always prepared a vegetarian dish for her. She had acquired a taste for avocado while living in California early in Mark's law career.

"Kidneys?" Aggie made a face.

"C'mon, you like kidney beans, dontcha?" coaxed Sissy, shoveling hers down like a starving waif.

"Dear, those aren't –" began Marybelle.

"Yes, these kidney beans are quite tasty," Maddy cut her off with a wink.

"Hmm, not bad," Aggie admitted after taking a teensy-weensy taste.

"Down the chute," encouraged N'yen," choosing not to enlighten either of the girls. With varied concoctions found in Vietnamese cooking, kidneys or kidney beans made no difference to him.

"About that Tristan Quilt," Leslie Ann picked up the thread of the earlier conversation. "Let's not forget that it is merely a fragment of a larger quilt. Two segments are already accounted for, one in the V&A, the other in the Bargello. So this leftover piece would be fairly small. It wouldn't take up a lot of space like a full-sized quilt or a wall hanging. It could be hidden in a small package."

"You make a very good point there," Maddy nodded. "It could be the size of a pillowcase."

"Say, you're pretty smart," said Sissy. "No need to be looking for an elephant when it's a mouse we want." Being from Alabama, she used a lot of aphorisms.

"Yes, we're looking for something little. Let's keep that in mind," said Aggie, reaching for another helping of steak and kidney pudding. Beans indeed!

"'It is, of course, a trifle, but there is nothing so important as trifles,'" said Leslie Ann.

Beau looked up from his plate. "That's a quote from Sherlock Holmes," he identified it. "From a short story, *The Man With the Twisted Lip.*"

"Right you are," she smiled. "Page 238, in fact."

"You certainly do know your Sherlock Homes."

"So do you."

"I'm a big fan of Arthur Conan Doyle. His writing, that is. His personal life was totally off the deep end."

"I've never noticed him to be off," responded Madame Flora, pausing a fork-skewed chunk of steak in midair. "He has been a very loyal spirit guide in my experience."

"Yes, well –"

"I find his support of spiritualism admirable," she huffed.

"I'm all for religious freedom," Beau mumbled.

"Mr. Conan Doyle was a very religious man," said Madame Flora, concluding the discussion. "He believed in an afterlife."

"Having read all his books, you must have been thrilled to meet Mr. Conan Doyle," Tilly said to her father. "Too bad he's a spirit these days and can't autograph them for you."

"Perhaps Madame Flora could use automatic writing to sign your books," suggested Aunt Hilda.

"Yes, that's where the spirit writes using her hand," explained Aunt Helga.

"I'd be happy to," agreed Madame Flora.

"Uh, thank you," said Beau, biting his tongue. He didn't want fake autographs marring his books.

There was a nervous titter around the dinner table, a roll of eyes, a polite cough – but no one spoke up. The table was divided into 4 believers versus 6 non-believer, enough differing opinions to spark a heated argument if not carefully checked.

"You know your Sherlock Holmes pretty good," Aggie said to Leslie Ann to change the topic from Arthur Conan Doyle's ethereal being. "Have you read all the books?"

"All 56 short stories and four novels," she quickly replied. Picking up on Aggie's keep-the-peace strategy.

"Didn't you used to be Leslie Ann Holmes?" asked Sissy. As was her habit in the old days, she had joined Aggie and N'yen for dinner at the Hoople Mansion. Like one of the family.

"I still am. Only my married name is now Trent."

"Are you related to Sherlock Holmes, having the same last name and all?"

Leslie Ann laughed, a sound like tinkling bells. "No such luck. The Great Detective isn't real. He was made up by Sir Arthur Conan Doyle, the man we were just talking about."

"The ghost?"

"Well, uh, yes. I suppose he would be a ghost now."

Sissy squinched up her face in consternation. "How come you folks are always quoting Sherlock Holmes if he's not real? Why listen to what a make-believe person has to say?"

"Sometimes authors say profound things through fictional characters in their books," Leslie Ann attempted to explain.

N'yen spoke up. "Sissy Jackson, you're going to have to read more if you're going to be my girlfriend. Broaden your horizons."

That stopped the conversation again.

Then Cecilia LaToya Jackson said, "Yes, Neesy. Can you recommend some good books?"

"Neesy?" sputtered Aggie.

Romance was in bloom.

Chapter Twelve

On the Ledge

Aunt Hilda looked pensive as she sipped her sherry after dinner that night. This had become a custom. Her wrinkled face had the contours of a dried apple. Without all the usual powder, rouge, and red lipstick, her sallow skin reminded you of an apple left to bake in the sun. "I'm sure some of our neighbors are werewolves, just waiting for the full moon before growing hair and baring fangs," she said to her sister.

"Which neighbors?" asked Aunt Helga. She looked around the room as if expecting someone to slip up behind her, a monster on the prowl. They were sitting in the ante-room, just outside their separate bedchambers. Being parsimonious by nature, they only had a few lights turned on, shrouding the area with shadows. No wonder it felt spooky to Helga.

They were an odd pair. If Aunt Hilda looked like Bette Davis in *What Ever Happened to Baby Jane*, Aunt Helga could have passed for a wizened Joan Crawford. But while constantly bickering, they were much less combative than the two movie stars had been, on or off screen.

"I'm not sure which neighbors," said Hilda, "but you have to admit it makes sense. If that Count Whatsizname was a werewolf, it's a chinch he bit someone else. And that person bit someone. After five generations it's a wonder that the whole town's not filled with werewolves."

"I see your point. But how do we identify them. They are not like vampires, unholy bloodsuckers that you can flush out with a cross or a clove of garlic."

"Wolfsbane," said Hilda.

"You mean that toxic European flowering plant?"

"The same – *Arnica montana* is the technical name."

"Maybe that would work, maybe not. I've heard it both ways. Some superstitious folks say werewolves can be repelled by the plant, or even tamed by it. Others believe that contact with wolfsbane on a full moon can turn you into a blood-crazed werewolf."

"Too risky?"

"I think so."

"Okay, then we'll use wormwood. Pungent-smelling silver-gray wormwood is said to ward off werewolves. Some people wear amulets of the leaves during Halloween as protection."

"Halloween?"

"Werewolves tend to come out more on All Hallows Eve."

"Wormwood – that's an ingredient of vermouth and absinthe," recalled Helga.

"All the better. We can drink martinis and ward off werewolves at the same time."

"Can we use it to identify those nasty shapeshifters?"

"Let me think," said Hilda. "Oh, I know. We could throw a big party where we serve drinks containing vermouth – manhattans, martinis, negronis, the Adonis, Americanos, Bronx cocktails, you name it. The wormwood in the vermouth will act as a detector. Anyone who refuses a drink is likely to be a werewolf in his or her human form."

"Her? Are there women werewolves too?"

"Don't be sexist, Helga. Get with the times. Being a bloodthirsty monster is an equal-opportunity career."

"Identifying them is one thing, but we may need some protection from them once we do. This could be very dangerous."

"Hmm. We'll have to research that," said Aunt Hilda. "Maybe we can get Agnes or N'yen to look it up on their computers for us. They are hooked into what's called the Information Super Highway."

"Agnes has her driver's license, so she might be a better bet on that Super Highway. N'yen's still waiting to take his test."

"Good point."

~ ~ ~

Around midnight, Aggie heard a scratching at her window. She sat up in bed, suddenly awake. What could it be? Her bedroom was on the third floor.

Her first thought was that it was a bat trying to get in, like Count Dracula making a house call. Then she remembered that scary scene in *Salem's Lot*, the movie based on a Stephen King novel. That scene where the vampire comes floating up outside the window, a Nosferatu-like monster looking for a drink of blood.

Aggie shook her head, making her blonde hair whip around her face like a Hydra, coming more fully awake. "What are you thinking?" she scolded herself. "You don't believe in vampires and werewolves and giant gorillas that climb the Empire State Building!"

Her dog Tige was growling at something. Even at 26 pounds, the fearless little wire-haired dachshund mix was a good watchdog.

Yes, there *was* something outside her window. She could make out the shape, like one of those gargoyles hunched on the cornerstones at Notre Dame. But that was impossible.

She felt around in the covers for her silver candlestick, but couldn't find it. Picking up a 10-pound dumbbell that she used for exercise – a girl had to watch her shape, didn't she? – she approached the glass where the silhouette loomed on the other side, three stories up on the side of the Hoople Mansion.

Spider-Man, she thought. More able to believe in a fictional superhero than a monster. She raised the dumbbell over her head as if it were a club. "Who's out there?" she called out.

"Me," came N'yen's voice. "Open the window and let me in."

Aggie unlatched the window and swung it inward. Rarely opened, it gave a creak like a stepped-on frog. "You idiot," she hissed. "What are you doing out there on the ledge?"

"A parapet connects the two cupolas. It leads right past your window," he said as he leapt into the safety of her room.

"That still doesn't answer my question: What are you doing out there?"

N'yen sighed. "I was trying to crawl over to the other cupola, the room where they hold the séances. I wanted to check it out for hidden microphones and such."

"Why didn't you just take the elevator up there and use the door. I doubt if it's locked."

He ducked his head, as if admitting cowardice. "That room is in the Hoople wing. You know we never go there unless invited. I didn't want Aunt Hilda or Aunt Helga catching me. I'd have to pass by their bedroom doors."

"Okay, I get that. But crawling along that ledge is crazy. You could have killed yourself. And I – and Sissy – wouldn't like that."

"Yeah, I get that now. I got scared halfway across – in front of your window as it turns out. Don't know what I would've done if you hadn't let me in."

The girl gave him a reproachful glare. "I almost didn't. I was dreaming it was a vampire or something out there. All that talk by the Hooples about werewolves got me spooked, I guess."

"That's silly," said N'yen. "We all know there's no such thing as werewolves."

"You know that, and I know that. But I'm not too sure about Sissy. If she had been here tonight, she would have probably stabbed you through the heart with a wooden stake."

"That's probably true," he agreed. "I've got to bring that girl into the 21st Century."

"Speaking of that … Neesy. Is she now your girlfriend?"

"Don't call me that. Only Sissy can get away with using that silly nickname. But, yes, I think we're going steady."

"Ha!" laughed Aggie. "Bet you're the only graduate student at Northwestern who's dating a 16-year-old."

"Yeah, but I'm only 16 myself."

"Still, that's going to be pretty awkward for double dates."

"Not if it's with you and Bobby Elwood."

Aggie blushed. But you couldn't make out the rosy cheeks in the darkened bedroom. "You might be embarrassed to be on a date with us. We're 18, y'know. Things can get pretty hot and heavy."

"Do you two –?"

"No. At least, not yet. But we're getting close."

"Really?"

"Don't you tell anyone, N'yen Madison, or next time I'll leave you out there on the ledge."

Chapter Thirteen

Online Shopping Spree

That next morning Aunt Hilda and Aunt Helga asked Aggie to help them with some online shopping.

"We're looking for a gift – perhaps a nice silver cross," said Hilda, exhibiting a smile like demented jack-o-lantern.

'Who's it for?" asked the teenager. Her suspicions rising.

"Uh, Rev. Kilroy," responded Helga. "His birthday's coming up."

"I'd think he would already have a cross. After all, he's a minister."

"One can't have too many crosses," snapped Helga. A little too quick in her response, confirming to Aggie that something was amiss with this out-of-the-blue shopping spree.

"What are you guys up to?" she demanded. "If you want my help, you'd better come clean."

Aunt Hilda looked shocked, or pretended to. "Why, dear, are you questioning our motives in buying a gift for our beloved minister?"

"I happen to know Rev. Kilroy celebrated his 47th birthday just last month. He announced it from the pulpit."

"Oh, we must have missed that service." The two women were erratic in their church attendance, always complaining of one malady or another.

"Spill your guts, or I'm closing my laptop and meeting N'yen at the library. He wants to check out their new books, particularly the astrophysics section."

"Is there a section devoted to that?" asked Aunt Helga.

"Probably not, but he thinks there should be. I'm sure he will have a book list for the new librarian."

"We've become friends with Dorothy Stargazer through the séances," chirped Aunt Hilda. "Perhaps we should give her a book list too."

"What kind of books do you have in mind?" asked Aggie, surprised by this off-the-wall suggestion.

"I was thinking about something on ways to combat werewolves."

"Zombie Apocalypses have become popular in fiction. Are you expecting a Werewolf Apocalypse?" laughed Aggie. These two old crones could be quite a giggle. She'd have to tell N'yen about this.

"Maybe not an Apocalypse," allowed Aunt Helga. "Just one or two instances."

"Perhaps a few small outbreaks," nodded Aunt Hilda.

"What's bringing this on? Too much sherry before bedtime?"

"Heaven forbids, child. Is that any way to speak to your elders?" said Hilda, fanning herself as if overwrought.

"Yes, no need to be rude," nodded Helga.

"Sorry," sighed Aggie, knowing she'd overstepped. "But where does this sudden concern about werewolves come from?"

Aunt Hilda replied shyly, "From the séance. Col. Madison said he shot that Count with a silver bullet. That meant he was trying to kill either a vampire or a werewolf, don't you agree?"

"That was nearly 200 years ago. People were more superstitious back then," Aggie dismissed their comments. She resented the fact that N'yen was at the library without her. And that Sissy was still home in bed while she was here talking crazy stuff about vampires and werewolves with her – what were they? – great-great aunts in name only.

"Indulge a couple of old ladies, will you, dear? Help us research ways to ward off werewolves and we will see that you're properly rewarded," wheedled Aunt Helga.

"Rewarded in what way?"

"We'll give you a quarter," proposed Aunt Hilda. Reaching for her purse. "No, make that fifty cents."

"Fifty cents? You can do better than that," laughed Aggie. "You two are loaded. And I'm one of your favorite pretend relatives."

"Okay, Agnes Tidemore, we'll put you in our will," offered Hilda. "How's that?"

"Really? I'd hoped I was already there."

"Nobody's there yet. Barney Solitairé has been trying to get us to put one together, but I can't decide who to give what to. Oh, your grandmother will get most of it – she being our next-in-line heir. But we want to leave a little something to all the family members. Problem is, we didn't have this make-believe family until the last few years, so we aren't prepared on how to divide things up."

"Okay, okay," joked Aggie. "I'll settle for a teensy weensy trust fund."

"But, my dear, your grandmother has already set one up for each of the grandchildren – you included."

"That's a college fund. I'm at Yale now and its very expensive. I won't have any left if I go to law school like my daddy did."

"Oh, you poor thing. Of course, you can have a trust fund. Now will you help us with our research?"

"Cool. Some ways to protect yourself from werewolves coming right up," she said, tapping at the keyboard of her Dell.

~ ~ ~

"Here's a good one," Aggie said, pointing at her computer screen. "A Werewolf Whistle – says it produces a sound higher than a Dog Whistle that's used by cryptozoologists to repel werewolves. This whistle emits a special supernatural ultrasonic sound that bothers both wolves and wolf-men."

"Oooo, let's see," Helga crowded closer to inspect the screen.

"You read it to us," instructed Hilda. Squinting at the display. "I forgot my reading glasses. Left them in the study, I think."

"No, the painting studio," said her sister. "You left them on the shelf on the easel."

"That can't be right. I had them this morning at breakfast. I was reading the newspaper."

"You're mistaken my dear. The *Burpyville Gazette* is an evening paper."

"Never mind that." She turned to Aggie. "What does the ad say?"

The advertisement was very descriptive of the device:

Werewolf Whistle
A Tool for Humans to Repel Werewolves

A small metal whistle of cylindrical shape that emits a supernatural sound undetectable by human ears, yet clearly audible to the paranormal werewolf ear. However it also emits a familiar whistling sound humans can hear so you know it's actually working. Those werewolf whistles with adjustable mechanisms can also be used for other paranormal creatures, and sometimes called by differing names depending on the default whistle adjustment. Such whistles are not the same as dog whistles, and are not recommended for use in repelling aggressive dogs, or other non-paranormal animals.

When blown the werewolf whistle will repel most werewolves, and a potentially a variety of other supernatural beings. This is due to the pain caused by the high pitched paranormal emissions of the life saving device that anyone can carry. Quality Werewolf Whistles are always calibrated by professional

Lycanthropologists or Cryptozoologists. Don't be left out in the cold of the dark paranormal night at the mercy of werewolves. Avoid getting close to these hairy horrors to utilize your holy water, silver daggers, crosses, and other holy artifacts. Don't chance the accuracy of your aim with a silver bullet loaded gun as a werewolf comes raging toward you. Get a Werewolf Whistle to repel these malevolent monsters before you even see them. The minute you hear an unholy howl just blow the Werewolf Whistle, and drive the damned denizens of destruction from your general vicinity. You can even blow it randomly as you venture out on full moon night to insure you don't get bitten and end up a victim of the Lycanthrope curse.

"Excellent," trilled Aunt Hilda. "Order two of those whistles. One for each of us. No, wait. Order one for every member of the family and the staff too. Even one for Lady Greystone. She'll be gone back to Jolly Old London by the time the whistles arrive, but we will forward one to her."

"A whistle's nice," decided Aunt Helga, "but I think we are going to need something stronger. What other options do we have?"

~ ~ ~

After a little searching, Aggie found a website titled *Ask Mystic Investigations*. It promised to provide "Paranormal Answers To Supernatural Questions." Perfect, she thought as she tapped on the computer keyboard.

As hoped, the website offered many suggestions on how to repel a werewolf. It listed the use of Holy Artifacts ranging from Crosses to Holy Water, Holy Fire to Holy Oil, or "just about anything blessed by a priest."

Holy Water was highly recommended, with the helpful hint that it could be loaded into a Super Soaker water gun to ward off attackers, or that you could wash your clothing in it to create a "protective shield" – although its power usually wears off after 24 hours, it warned.

"Holy Water, that ought to do it," said Hilda. "Where can we get some?"

"At a church?" guessed Aggie. She'd already concluded these old ladies were totally looney.

"Good idea," nodded Aunt Helga. "Let's go see Rev. Kilroy. I'll bet he has a big supply."

"Are you sure this is a good idea?" cautioned Aggie. She could imagine these two old ladies being locked away in a rubber room if they went around town looking for Holy Water to repel werewolves.

"It's an excellent idea," sniffed Aunt Hilda. "And probably less expensive than a Werewolf Whistle." Despite being immensely wealthy, these two children of the Post Great Depression years were incredibly cheap.

"Thank you, Agnes," nodded Aunt Helga. "I'll have to learn how use one of these machines someday." She nodded at the Dell Latitude 3310 laptop that Aggie used for her classes at Yale.

"Yes, you should," replied Aggie. But she was thinking about the dangers of these crazy old women being set loose on Facebook or other websites where their deranged theories and unfounded gossip could possibly do harm.

"Alright, we're off to see the Wizard," said Aunt Hilda, dangling the car keys between two boney fingers.

"You mean the Minister," corrected her sister. She adjusted a pillbox hat on her gray hair, ready to go.

"You're not supposed to be driving," cautioned Aggie. Knowing their driver's licenses had expired years ago.

"Oh, don't you worry, dear. Driving a car is like falling off a horse. You never forget how to do it once you learn."

~ ~ ~

Rev. James Noah Kilroy was working on Sunday's sermon when the Hoople sisters showed up at his small office at the rear of Pleasant Meadows. The church was magnificent in its simplicity, white clapboard with a shingle roof and tall, pointed spire. The interior consisted of a nave lined with hardwood pews and a pulpit positioned in front of a baptismal font. Over the font was a stained-glass window depicting Jesus and sheep and little children. There was a stairwell on one side of the church leading down to a basement where Sunday School classes took place.

Unlike the ornate Catholic Cathedral over in Burpyville, there was no transept (a traverse aisle crossing the nave in front of the sanctuary in a cruciform church) or chancel, no vestry where the robes were stored, no confessional booths off to the side. And no font of Holy Water stationed near the front entrance.

Rev. Kilroy's office at the back of the church was barely big enough for a polished oak desk with three leather-backed chairs and a narrow bookcase filled with religious tracts.

"Ladies, what can I do for you on this blessed day?" the minister greeted his guests. They were VIPs in his estimation, the Hooples having given generous donations to Pleasant Meadows over the years. He worried that the generosity of the Hoople Quadruplet Trust Fund would dry up with their eventual passing. They were in their late 80s, if they were day. So he said, "Are you here to make another bequest to the church?"

"No, not today. We simply want to purchase a couple gallons of Holy Water," announced Aunt Hilda. "We have some plastic gas cans in the back seat of our car. We stopped by Home Depot on the way over here."

"H-holy Water?"

"That's right. Sanctified water that has been blessed by the church. That would be you, I guess."

73

"What do you need with so much Holy Water? Are you planning a baptism ceremony of some sort? Should I be prepared to officiate?"

"No, no. Nothing like that," Aunt Helga clicked her tongue to dismiss the thought. "We need it for our protection."

"From Satan?"

"No," Aunt Hilda shook her head. "From werewolves."

Rev. Kilroy frowned. "What? Surely you can't be serious. Werewolves aren't real. They are the imaginary creations of superstitions and Hollywood movies."

"Now, now," said Helga. "You don't have to be so protective of us. We know the town's riddled with shapeshifters – posing as ordinary family men by day, but transforming into howling monsters by the light of a full moon."

"Is this some kind of joke?" He stared at the two women as if expecting them to break into a laugh at their fine prank. They almost had him going there.

"Oh, we're very serious. We just feel foolish that we've gone all these years without realizing the threat which surrounds us. You should have clued us in."

"I think he tried," said Hilda's sister. "All those sermons about Satan and the Legends of Hell, we just didn't realize what he was really talking about."

"Acts 20:29," quoted Hilda. "Paul said, *"After my departure fierce wolves will come in among you, not sparing the flock.'"*

"Yes, and Matthew 7:15," added Helga. "Jesus warned us to *'beware of false prophets, who come to you in sheep's clothing but inwardly are ravenous wolves.'* "

"And what about King Nebuchadnezzar? In the 4th chapter of Daniel, it says, *'And he was driven from men, and did eat grass as oxen, and his body was wet with the dew of heaven, till his hairs were grown like eagles', and his nails like birds'.* That sure sounds like a werewolf to me."

"Ladies, you have this all wrong. There are no werewolves in the Bible, just wolves. And Holy Water is not used to chase monsters, real or imagined. I ask you to sit down and get your breath. I will break out a cup of sacrament wine for each of you, maybe one for myself." Unlike Baptist churches that substituted grape juice for actual wine in the Communion ceremony, Rev. Kilroy believed in using the real thing. He kept an ample supply of Mogen David in a wine cabinet behind the baptismal font.

"Yes, thank you," accepted Hilda. "Wine seems like a fine idea." She had a habit of imbibing sherry before bedtime, and had developed quite a taste.

"Maybe just sip," agreed Helga. "Then we can fill up our plastic cans with Holy Water. You've got plenty of it in that big baptismal font over there."

Chapter Fourteen

Medieval Quilt Fragments

At that same moment Beau Madison and Lizzie's husband Edgar were surrounded by lots of water, fishing for striped bass on the Wabash River. Common fish caught there included white bass, striped bass, hybrid striped bass, smallmouth bass, spotted bass, and largemouth bass, not to mention catfish. Beau and Edgar Ridenour were using eel as bait. Some days stripers will eat any live bait you throw at them, and other days they'll go after only one specific type of bait.

They used a 10-pound test line with a smaller 6/0 circle hook. Both preferred Ugly Stik Striper Rods for their durability. Built from a blend of graphite and fiberglass, you can bend an Ugly Stik right over on itself and they won't break. They were well suited for close-in work on a boat.

Beau and Edgar co-owned a 20-foot Roughneck 2070 SC. With a 24-inch side depth, the boat could handle the uncertain depths of the Wabash. Although navigable by large ships in the past, much of the river has become shallow due to erosion and silt. What's more, the Roughneck's variable-deadrise V-hull delivered a smooth, dry ride.

When N'yen was here, he usually went fishing with his Grampy and Uncle Edgar. He was technically the better fisherman of the three, despite his young age. They were surprised when the boy turned them down today, choosing to go to a Quilters Club meeting.

"Think he's turning into a sissy?" asked Edgar, worried about this lack of enthusiasm for fishing today. That was unlike N'yen.

"Sissy is the right word," chuckled Beau. "I think the kid has a crush on Sissy Jackson."

"Buck's granddaughter?"

"One and the same?"

Edgar ran his hand thoughtfully through his bushy beard. Since retiring, the one-time banker had quit shaving and now looked like a Jerimiah Johnson mountain man. "Well, that's understandable," he said. "I remember a time when you and I would've chosen a pretty girl over a striped bass."

"True, although we met our wives at a young age."

"My point exactly. When I met Lizzie – I'll never forget that day in high school – I gave up fishing till I retired."

"You've certainly made up for it since then," Beau nudged his pal. "I don't see how you eat all the fish you catch."

"Give most of them away. Lizzie's not much on cooking."

"We eat all of my catches. There are a lot of mouths to feed in the Hoople Mansion. And Marybelle oversees two cooks."

"Lucky guy, living in the lap of luxury."

"C'mon, your wife is rich. She's the biggest stockholder in the Savings and Loan. You could afford a cook."

Edgar waved away his friend's words and changed the subject. He preferred a simple life. "What's going on at the Quilters Club that has them meeting today? They usually get together on Tuesday afternoons."

"I expect it has to do with that message from the séance. They hope to find the quilt that my great-grandfather's ghost was talking about."

"Your great-grandfather's ghost? You don't believe that stuff, do you?"

"Naw, I know it's all baloney. But for the life of me, I can't figure out how that Madame Flora – or her spirits – found out about the silver bullet. That's been a closely held family secret for generations."

"What *is* the story on that silver bullet? Was your ancestor shooting vampires?"

Beau shrugged sheepishly. "Just about. According to the story handed down through time, he shot a werewolf."

"No kidding?"

"I'd just as soon believe in ghosts as werewolves. But that's the way the story goes. I'm only telling you now that that so-called spirit spilled the beans."

"Why the big secret?"

"C'mon, Edgar. I saw the way you looked at me when I said 'werewolf.' We Madisons didn't want people thinking we were nuts."

"Then why pass along the story to future generations?"

"It's the silver bullet that gets passed along, more than the story. You see, it was my great-grandfather's wedding ring, a family heirloom. I guess we Madisons are, at the core, a sentimental lot."

~ ~ ~

N'yen was impressed by the town's new librarian. Dorothy Stargazer had put together a good selection of books on astrophysics and astronomy. A least for a beginner in the fields. He ticked them off his list:

- *An Introduction to Astrophysics* by Baidyanath Basu;
- *Schaum's Outline on Astronomy* by Stacey Palen;
- *An Introduction to the Study of Stellar Structure* by S. Chandrasekhar;
- *Theoretical Astrophysics* by T. Padmanabhan;
- *Seven Brief Lessons on Physics* by Carlo Rovelli;
- *A Brief History of Time* by Stephen Hawking;
- *Relativity: The Special and General Theory* by Albert Einstein;
- *An Introduction to Galaxies And Cosmology* by Mark Jones, Robert Lambourne, and Stephen Serjeant; and

- *Hyperspace: A Scientific Odyssey Through Parallel Universes, Time Warps, and the Tenth Dimension* by Michio Kaku.

"Not bad, but you need to add one more," he said.

"What?"

"*Cosmos* by Carl Sagan."

"That's not a very technical book."

"No, it's poetry. At least to a scientist."

"I'll put it on order," she agreed. Dorothy Stargazer might believe in séances and ghosts, but she was a good librarian.

"Thanks."

Just then Aggie rushed in. "N'yen, we have to find Grammy," she said in near-panic.

"What's wrong?" he asked. No longer thinking of books. "Is she all right?

"It's not her," she exclaimed. "It those lunatic aunts – Hilda and Helga. They've gone bonkers."

N'yen let out his breath. "Whew, you scared me for a moment. I thought something was wrong."

"Didn't you hear what I just said? Those old cuckoos have gone off the deep end. They're out hunting werewolves!"

"Big deal. My silver platter is on my nightstand. I've got several cans of Pepsi and a giant bag of Cheetos sitting on it."

"Get serious. They are out looking for Holy Water."

"What brought this on? Is it a full moon?" he jibed. He didn't take the old women seriously.

"No, it was that ghost at the séance talking about killing the Count with a silver bullet. Now they think there's a werewolf invasion."

"Did you say werewolves?" asked Dorothy Stargazer.

"That's right," laughed N'yen. "Like Lon Chaney Jr. in those old Universal horror movies. Or Jack Nicholson in *Wolf*."

"That makes sense – a werewolf," said the librarian.

"You don't believe that garbage, do you?"

"I was at the séance. Col. Madison shot that man with a silver bullet. I heard him say so myself."

N'yen was surprised to hear Dorothy Stargazer – the librarian who had compiled such a rational list of books on astronomy and astrophysics – spouting such nonsense. He turned to his cousin. "Do you believe that werewolf stuff?"

"Of course not," Aggie replied. "But the point is, Hilda and Helga Hoople do. And so does my mom. And I'm not so sure about Grampy."

Chapter Fifteen

British Royalty on Display

L eslie Ann Trent (née Holmes) might be a member of British royalty, married to an earl and all, but she was still that same bright sleuth who back in 2002 had helped the Quilter Club solve that mystery of a patchwork quilt based on a Thomas Nast drawing of Father Christmas. (See Book 7.)

That had been a good year – her year abroad as a Hands Across the Sea exchange student in America. She looked back on it fondly. Even today, she still considered Maddy and Beau Madison like a second family.

Her husband Oliver – Lord Oliver officially – was veddy veddy British. He teased her that she was a "Yankee at heart" – though no one in the American Midwest would describe themselves as Yankees. That was more of a description for the people of New England, not Indiana. But he was right – a piece of Leslie Ann's heart lay in the Hoosier State.

She had met Oliver at university. They both attended Oxford. He had studied diplomacy and foreign affairs in the Department of Politics and International Relations. She had concentrated on British literature, particularly The Romantic Period (1785–1832).

The Earl of Greystone had been her Prince Charming, although she certainly didn't need "saving." She didn't subscribe to the Cinderella Complex, the idea that a woman "is not capable of changing her situations with her own actions and must be helped by an outside force, usually a male (i.e., the Prince)."

Leslie Ann was headstrong and independent, almost too much so for the duties that go with royalty. Princess Diana had faced that problem. So had Fergie. So had Meghan.

Her husband would have advised her to stay out of American affairs, but here she was, conspiring with her friends to something illegal. They were going to rob a bank.

They just didn't know it yet.

~ ~ ~

Beau didn't really believe there was a quilt fragment, a prize waiting to be found right here in Caruthers Corners. The idea of a rare Italian museum piece being hidden here in a remote corner of the Midwest stretched credulity. Sure, his wife and the Quilters Club gals were all atwitter over this phantom quilt, but they tended to get excitable over old scraps of cloth and such.

His theory was that this was some kind of blackmail scheme, a threat to discredit his ancestor, Beauregard the First. Pay up or else face disgrace!

After all, Col. Madison had shot the Count dead *after* the duel was over, a bullet to the heart of an unarmed man. Not very sporting. Or legal.

Worse still was that this revered Town Founder had thought he was killing a werewolf. Of all the crazy things! Instead of a brave visionary who led a wagon train west, his legacy would be that of a lunatic murderer.

Yes, it had to be a blackmail scheme. For what other reason would the "spirit" have mentioned the silver bullet?

Sharing this thought with Police Chief Jim Purdue, he and Jim were just waiting for the shoe to drop – Madame Flora asking for money. Then she would be staring at bars from inside a jail cell.

Chapter Sixteen

Wormwood

"**D**id you send out the invitations?" Aunt Hilda asked Marybelle. Aside from overseeing the household staff, the Brit also acted as secretary for the dotty old duo.

"Just as you asked," came the reply in that posh accent that reminded you of Julie Andrews or Princess Margaret. Or Lady Greystone. "Two hundred invitations to your garden party went out this morning."

"And did you order the liquor – especially the vermouth?"

"Indeed I did. I've also engaged four bartenders and eight wait staff. Our own kitchen helpers will prepare an assortment of hors d'oeuvre."

"What would we ever do without you?" said Helga.

"Can I wear my fairy wings to the party?" asked Tilly. "They are ever so fashionable."

"If you like, my dear," said Hilda.

"Or you could be a butterfly," said Helga.

"How about that new gown you bought last week at Spitzers in Burpyville?" suggested Marybelle. "You'd look like the belle of the ball."

"That sounds perfect," smiled Tilly.

"Did you get a permit to hold the garden party in the Town Square?" asked Hilda. "The one inconvenient thing about living up here on top of Hoople Hill is that our yard is so very small. Two hundred people would never fit."

"Tilly's husband has taken care of that," Marybelle assured her. "The mayor has to sign off on all rentals of public property in any case."

"Remember, the drink menu is very strict," said Helga.

"That's right," echoed Hilda. "No wine, no beer, no specialty drinks. No sodas, no tea. Only the ones on our list."

"I notice that all of them contain vermouth," said Marybelle.

"Yes, it's a theme party," replied Hilda.

"Remember, we only want Cocchi Dry Vermouth di Torino Limited Edition," said Helga. "We've done our research. It's pricy but worth every penny."

~ ~ ~

Cocchi Vermouth di Torino is at least 15% along with wormwood, cinchona bark, rhubarb, orange peel, gentian, star anise, yarrow, rose petal, juniper, quassia, nutmeg, coriander, sandalwood, musk, and myrrh. The high wormwood content cinched the deal.

In the USA, many vermouths are made without wormwood because FDA legislation stipulates that the finished beverage must be free of thujone, a compound considered by the authorities to be psychoactive and toxic in large doses. Thujone is present in notable amounts in wormwood, as well as other bittering agents.

In Europe, vermouth production is highly regulated, and while there's no hard and fast rule about which grapes can be used to make it, at least 75% by volume must be wine. And by EU law, vermouth must contain *Artemisia*.

Vermouth derives its name from the German *wermut* and the French *vermout*, which translate to "wormwood." To meet the European definition of vermouth, at least one of the many species of wormwood (*Artemisia spp.*) is required to be included in the recipe.

There is currently only one geographical designation for vermouth recognized by law: Vermouth di Torino. To qualify, the vermouth must be produced in Piedmont Italy using only Italian wine. It must be between 16% ABV and 22% ABV, mainly bittered with wormwood (*Artemisia absinthium*), and its sweeteners are limited to sugar, grape must, caramel, and honey.

Yes, Cocchi Vermouth di Torino was the brand of choice when it came to scaring off werewolves.

Chapter Seventeen

Rare Manuscripts

Heinrich Bashinski had a gift for coming up with marks – suckers who would fall for his cons. He'd come up with the Hoople family by connecting the dots. Those crazy old ladies had a niece who was a big quilter. And the niece had a loopy daughter who would buy into the Fortune Telling scam, a perfect patsy. The question was what could he use as a hook?

A visit to the Perricock Museum of Science & History had given him the answer: The niece's husband was a descendent of a Town Founder. Yes, a visit from the spirit of Col. Beauregard Hollingsworth Madison was in order. That would get their attention.

But what could the spirit of Col. Madison bring up that would make believers of them? What would convince them to fork over a million bucks?

He had found the answer at Robert's Rare Hoosier-Only Autographs & Manuscripts Emporium, a small shop located on an out-of-the-way side street in Indianapolis. The proprietor, a dour man named Robert Bob Roberts, was a great source of Indiana memorabilia – autographs of such natives as Abraham Lincoln, William Henry Harrison, James Whitcomb Riley, James Dean, Cole Porter, Kurt Vonnegut, David Letterman, Mike Pence, Wilbur Wright, Michael Jackson, even Colonel Sanders (who was born in Henryville, Indiana, not Kentucky). And there were rare documents as well – ranging from rambling letters by Theodore Dreiser to lyrics written by Hoagy Carmichael on the back of a napkin, a portion of a diary by Squire Boone (Daniel's brother) to signed publicity photographs of a young Janet Jackson, even a love note from Steve McQueen to Ali McGraw, and the word POTATOE handwritten on a prompt card by Dan Quayle.

What a cornucopia of nearly forgotten Hoosier history!

When Heinrich asked him for something related to the Founding Fathers of Caruthers Corners, Indiana, the manuscript dealer had to give it some thought. That was a tiny middle-of-nowhere town to the north. But he was sure he had a few relevant pieces somewhere in his overstuffed filing cabinets. After a few hours searching, Robert Bob Roberts came up with seven items:

1. A faded tintype photograph of Jacob Abernathy Caruthers, Ferdinand Aloysius Jinks, and Col. Beauregard Hollingsworth Madison. Photographer and date unknown.

2. A first printing of Jacob Caruthers' journal titled *My Journey into Indian Territory, 1829*. Annotated by his descendant, Henry Caruthers, a former mayor of Caruthers Corners.

3. A *carte de visite* picturing Ferdinand Jinks in a morning suit. Photographed by Alexander Gardner circa 1863.

4. The Last Will and Testament of Major Samuel Elmsford Beasley. He left everything to his dog, Rover. But his family overturned his last wishes.

5. A handwritten sermon by Rev. Thaddeus Barrington Taylor. It assured his parishioners they were all going to Hell.

6. A letter by Count Antonio Guicciardini. Returned to Sender.

7. A yellowed newspaper obituary from *Indiana Gazette* for Sir Samuel Langston Buttersworth, shot dead in a duel with one Mordicai Bradshaw in an argument over a lame horse. Dated August 2, 1830.

"Any of these do the trick?" asked Robert Bob Roberts. He knew what Heinrich did for a living. He dealt with several crooks, forgers, and con men. He'd sold stuff to Heinrich before – no questions asked.

Heinrich Bashinski studied the scattering of documents and photographs there on the glass-topped table. "Hmm, maybe the will or the obit," he muttered doubtfully.

"Take a look at the letter."

He did.

"What's the Tristan and Isolde Quilt?" he said.

Chapter Eighteen

Tristan and Isolde

Sir Thomas Mallory's *Le Morte d'Arthur* told the chivalric story of King Arthur and the Knights of the Round Table. But British literature offers several other tales of medieval knights and their quests: *Sir Gawain and the Green Knight, Lanzelet, Merlin,* and *Percival, the Story of the Grail.*

The romance of *Tristan and Isolde* was one of these. It described the adulterous affair between the knight Tristan (Tristram, etc.) and the princess Isolde (Iseult, Yseult, among other spellings). In addition to the English version, the story has its counterparts in Ireland, Persia, France, Italy, various Slavic countries, Spain, and even in Old Norse. All differing slightly.

However, the images on the two fragments of the Triston Quilt came from another source. Researchers agree the quilt's depictions more closely follow the narrative of chapters 17–19 of a 14th-Century novella called *La Tavola Rotonda o L'Istoria di Tristano.* This is a medieval illuminated manuscript that gives "the histories of the Round Table, and of Sir Tristan and Sir Lancelot and of many other knights." Preserved at the National Central Library of Florence, the manuscript bears the date of 20 July 1446. It was made by the copyist Zuliano degli Anzoli and his collaborators. A work of great literary and artistic value, the *Ritonda* panels include 289 illustrations almost entirely drawn in pen.

La Tavola Rotonda o L'Istoria di Tristano tells about the oppression of Cornwall by Languis of Ireland and his champion Amoroldo (a variation on "Morholt"), and the battle of Tristan on behalf of King Mark of Cornwall. But its main theme is the triangular relationship between the knight, the princess, and the king – not unlike the conflicted romance of Sir Lancelot, Queen Guinevere, and King Arthur.

The iconography on the quilt depicts the story in large squares. Seeing a picture on Google, N'yen described it as being similar to the panels of a modern comic book.

~ ~ ~

"I've consulted some of my quilting histories," said Lizzie Ridenour. She had a very good reference library at the Hoople Quilting Heritage Museum, thanks to a generous grant by the Hoople Quadruplets Trust. 'What we're looking for may actually be a fourth fragment, rather than a third."

"What? I thought this was supposed to be the rarest quilt in the world," said Bootsie.

"It is," replied the redhead. "Well, when it comes to medieval quilts."

"That's right," nodded Cookie. Turning on her eidetic memory, she cited:

> "The oldest known actual whole cloth European quilts are three trapunto, or stuffed quilts from Italy. Two, the so-called Guicciardini quilts, were probably made for a Florentine wedding in the 1390's (and may have originally been a wall-hanging), while a third seems to have been an actual coverlet. All are made with the same materials (linen top and back, cotton padding, linen thread) and with the same technique (dark brown backstitched outlines on the decorative motifs, running stitch on the backgrounds). The iconography and the motifs are so similar that these items were all but certainly made in the same workshop, while the designs and the captions on the Guicciardini quilts are in an otherwise rare Sicilian dialect."

"So what's this about a third fragment?" asked Bootsie.
"Is that the one we're looking for?" asked Aggie.

"No, I'm talking about the first third fragment," said Lizzie.

"Actually, it's not a fragment," corrected Cookie. "It's a full-sized quilt … or most of one. Experts believe it comes from the same atelier as the Tristan Quilt, but was never a part of it."

"That's right," nodded Lizzie. "I'm referring to what's known as the Pianetti Quilt. It's now missing, but early photos show a central medallion with Tristan and Isolde displayed on a field of fleur de lis."

She read from her reference book:

> "Less well known is the third quilt, which was owned by the Pianetti family. This piece, only half of which was extant when it was last photographed, once again showed Tristan and Isolde, only in central medallion surrounded by heavily stuffed fleur-de-lis. The border shows allegorical figures feasting in vineyards and gardens, but there are no captions so the meaning is not clear."

Cookie picked up the story. "Some authorities believe the Guicciardini quilts were originally a wall hanging that was subsequently altered into two coverlets. Ultraviolet light tests on the Bargello quilt show traces of calcium on the back side, which could have come from its use as a wall hanging."

She gave the dimensions: "The V&A quilt measures approximately 10 ½ feet high by 9 ½ feet wide. The Bargello quilt measures slightly larger than 8 feet high by about 6 ¾ feet wide. However, textile historian Sarah Randles argues that the two quilt fragments were originally parts of one large quilt, which measured about 19 feet high by 13 feet wide. That would mean significant sections are missing.

"Maybe this lost fragment is one of them," suggested Maddy.

"That makes sense," nodded Bootsie.

Cookie continued with the description. "The two known fragments of the Tristan Quilt illustrate parts of the Tristan and Isolde story. Randles postulates that the scenes were arranged clockwise on the border, with the central images paired and reading bottom to top. There are six scenes in the central section of the V&A quilt, with a border of four-leaf clovers. The Bargello quilt has eight scenes that portray Tristan leaving his foster-father's court to go to King Mark of Cornwall; the meeting of Tristan with Morholt for combat; and their fight on horseback."

Lizzie added the technical details: "The quilt is made from two layers of linen, stitched together with wadding in between. A backstitch in cream and brown linen thread defines a series of pictures with captions that have been brought into relief by inserting rolls of cotton stuffing to raise sections of the design, a technique known as trapunto. The stuffing could have been introduced during the quilting process, or because the backing layer is looser in weave, its threads could have been parted to introduce the stuffing."

Lizzie explained that these quilts are thought to have been made for a wedding between two powerful Florentine families around 1394. "But it's been pointed out that this Sicilian retelling of the story of Tristan and Isolde seems strangely inappropriate for a wedding gift, especially if the quilt was indeed intended for use on the bridal bed."

Whether there was originally one quilt intended for an enormous ceremonial bed, a set of two quilts meant for two beds, or a huge wall hanging is not known, she added. "But it's pretty clear that the so-called Pianetti Quilt was an entirely separate creation."

"So where is that third quilt?" asked Aggie.

Lizzie said, "The Pianetti Quilt was last seen in 1938. It has vanished without a trace, leading to the tragic conclusion that it was lost during the massive destruction that occurred during World War II."

"Or that it's hidden away in a private collection," Leslie Ann interjected.

"A private collection?" said Lizzie, as if the thought had never occurred to her.

"You'd be surprised what some of the old European families have hidden away from the public," nodded Leslie Ann. "Along with my husband, I've been inside a number of old castles and manor homes throughout Europe. It's amazing what you come across. I've seen a Leonardo Da Vinci that's not even on the list of his known paintings."

"Where does this stuff come from?" asked Sissy.

"Some of these objets d'art have been in families for generations, some acquired by private collectors, and some – shamefully – were confiscated by Nazis during World War II."

"I've seen *Monuments Men*, that movie about those soldiers who reclaimed a lot of stolen art after World War II," said Bootsie. "George Clooney and Bill Murray recovered a lot of those missing masterpieces."

"And *Lady in Gold*," added Aggie. "That's the one where a painting of Helen Mirren was stolen by Nazis and winds up in a museum in Vienna, Austria."

"The painting was actually a portrait of Adele Bloch-Bauer I by Gustav Klimt. In the movie Helen Mirren played her niece, who sued the museum for the return of the stolen painting," corrected Maddy.

"So there are a lot of paintings and such hidden away in private collections," sighed Sissy. "So what?"

"Yeah, that's all sort of beside the point," agreed N'yen. "You said we're looking for a valuable quilt that was hidden away around here in the early 1800s."

"Right," Lizzie nodded, getting back on track. "Question is, where should we start looking?"

"Beats me," admitted Cookie.

"I don't have a clue," enjoined Bootsie."

"Dunno," shrugged Maddy.

"Divide and conquer," suggested Leslie Ann. Quick with a plan of action.

"How so?"

"Work in pairs," she suggested. "Cookie and Bootsie search the old records for anything they can find out about this Count Antonio Guicciardini. There have to be more historical records about him. Can you turn up the actual death certificate? An address where he lived? Any mention of him in old newspapers?"

"And me?" asked Lizzie.

"You and I will try to find out more details about this quilt fragment. How did it come into the possession of Count Guicciardini? Where was he taking it? We might have to go down to the big library in Burpyville to research its history. Right now, we don't even know for sure that a piece of the Tristan Quilt actually came to Caruthers Corners. We only have the word of a questionable spirit from a séance – not the best of authorities."

"How about me?" N'yen tugged at her sleeve. His eagerness showing.

"You and Sissy make a list of good hiding places around town. Places we can check out."

"But I'm new to town," protested Sissy. "And so is N'yen compared to you Quilters Club ladies. You've lived here all your lives." She made that sound like a long, long time.

"True," smiled Maddy. "But if you can start the list with all the logical places you can think of, we'll all come together and see what we can add."

"Logical places?" said Sissy. "You mean like a bank's safe deposit boxes?"

"The Caruthers Corners Savings and Loan wasn't around in the early 1800s," Lizzie spoke up. She ought to know. Her grandfather founded the bank.

"See? I told you I didn't know my way 'round,'" muttered Sissy.

"Maybe places like the old Caruthers Mansion," N'yen put on his thinking cap. "It's now the E-Z Seat Chair Factory. Or a tomb in the Old Section of Pleasant Glade Cemetery."

"That's the idea," encouraged Maddy.

"How about you?" asked Leslie Ann. "What do you want to take on?"

Maddy didn't hesitate with an answer. "Aggie and I will work on my husband Beau, try to get him to tell us more of the story about his great-grandfather and this silver bullet that supposedly killed Count Guicciardini. I suspect there's something he's holding back."

Chapter Nineteen

"Went to a Garden Party ..."

The Hoople Quadruple Garden Party was a huge success. Free drinks and a large selection of finger food was enough to lure out the majority of the 200 invitees.

That afternoon the Town Square looked quite festive with strings of twinkling lights and milling crowds and the sound of bouncy music.

Thanks to the proven efficacy of the Mod-Tim coronavirus vaccine, no one worried that this would be a super spreader event. The entire town – 100% – had participated in a Modern Times vaccine test. Even so, most people wore masks except when they were imbibing.

There were two bars, with two bartenders each. Hilda stationed herself at one; Helga at the other. They were looking for people who refused to drink the vermouth-laden cocktails. Those who avoided the wormwood might be werewolves.

Some folks had a seemingly legitimate excuse to refuse one of the free cocktails:

Janey Baumgartner was pregnant again.

Ed McGonigal and Louis Pascal were attending AA.

Rev Kilroy was a professional teetotaler. Except for communion wine.

Rita Rutaberger was on some kind of medication that didn't allow her any alcohol.

Old Tom Dancy was off the sauce following a DUI.

Deputy Harry Teague was on duty.

And several others.

Jasper Beanie, the Town Hall custodian and Pleasant Glade caretaker, crashed the party. His uninhibited drinking was making up for the ones who abstained. He certainly earned his reputation as the "town drunk." He would spend the night sleeping it off in his familiar jail cell, like that fat guy Otis in those old *Andy Griffith* TV shows.

Standing next to the bars, Aunt Hilda and Aunt Helga held clipboards on which they marked down the status of each person at the party. Of 200 invitations, 176 showed up. Plus Jasper. It was unclear what they were going to do with their list of "werewolves" once the party was over. It wasn't practical to shoot each one with a silver bullet. And the two elderly women didn't have the stamina to go around town driving stakes into people's hearts.

"We should have thought ahead," Hilda whispered in her sister's ear. The music was loud – they'd hired Paul Whittaker and his Hoosier Hotshots as entertainment for the party.

"In what way?"

"We could have served a special punch to all the non-drinkers. A concoction like Rev. Jim Jones's Kool-Aid. That would have taken care of all those wolf-men in one fell swoop."

"You would have got a few innocent people too. Like Janey Baumgartner and Rev. Kilroy."

"That's what the Pentagon calls 'collateral damage.' Deaths that can't be helped."

Leslie Ann was on the bandstand introducing each number by the Hoosier Hotshots. They were doing their oldies-but-goodies playbook. "When I Fall in Love," "I Only Have Eyes for You," "Our Love Is Here to Stay," "Memories Are Made of This," songs like that.

Billy Hofstadter caught her off guard when he walked up and asked her to dance. Now the manager of the T-Mobile store, Billie had dated Leslie Ann some 18 years ago when she was the young exchange student staying with the Madisons.

"May I have this dance?" he said shyly.

"Billy, is that you?" she asked, trying to replace the receding hairline with the shaggy locks of his youth in her mind's eye.

"None other," he grinned. "I heard you were in town for a visit."

"Yes, my husband – the Earl of Greystone – had business in Indianapolis," she said, getting it on record that she was now a married lady – even a Lady in the formal sense of the word.

"I heard you'd added a title to your name. I'm not surprised. I always thought you were pretty enough to be a princess."

"Actually I'm only a countess – but who's quibbling. I asked Maddy about you. She said you were in the telecommunications industry."

Billy blushed. "Well, just barely. I manage the T-Mobile store on South Main. You can see it from here," he pointed toward a line of brick-fronted buildings.

"Very impressive. Let's have that dance. The song the Hoosier Hotshots are playing – 'It's Only Make Believe,' that was one of our favorites."

"Just like old times."

"Not quite," she said, holding up her ring finger to remind him.

~ ~ ~

The next day Aunt Hilda said, "I think I've got one."

"Got what?" asked her sister.

"I've identified a local werewolf. Plain as the nose on your face."

Aunt Helga looked up from her sewing. She was quite talented when it came to making patchwork quilts. Her works had been exhibited at the Hoople Quilting Heritage Museum. She was working on a Double Wedding Ring pattern. "Who, pray tell?"

103

"Benjamin Bentley."

"Cookie Bentley's husband?"

"One and the same, sister dear. He was on our list of people who did not drink at the garden party. He was obviously avoiding vermouth, which contains wormwood. That's proof positive."

"Several people didn't drink."

"They're all under suspicion,' snapped Hilda. "But we must deal with them one at a time. We can't take on an entire pack of these beasts."

"Cookie said he wasn't drinking because he's taking Cardura for his high blood pressure. You're not supposed to mix a doxazosin and alcohol. It can cause heart arrhythmia, I'm told."

"That's just what his wife is saying to cover up for his affliction. Take a look at him, sister. The man is squat like an animal. And powerful. Remember, as a boy he was the State Wrestling Champion. And have you ever seen him working in the fields without his shirt? He's as hairy as a dog."

"Well, you're right about that," said Helga. "I've seen him mowing hay. He's as hairy as that James Bond actor, Sean Connery."

"Connery's one too. But he's dead now, so there's not much point in digging him up to prove it."

"I think that Hugh Jackman's a werewolf too. And he's alive."

"No, he plays a wolverine in the movies. Despite the similar names, a wolverine is actually a member of the weasel family. I looked it up."

"Back to Ben Bentley," said Helga. "What do we do about him? I don't like the idea of him crawling in our window one night."

"That would not be good," nodded her sister. Ignoring the fact that their bedrooms were on the third floor of the Hoople

Mansion, a prison-like structure with vertical stone walls. "We must do something about Ben Bentley."

"What?"

"Sprinkle him with our Holy Water. That should break the spell, free him from his curse."

"Are you sure about this? I'd hate to throw water in his face only to discover that it's not as Holy as we think."

"You're suggesting –?"

"Everybody knows Rev. Kilroy had a fling with Bitsy Smoot a few years ago. He repented and all that. But what if that weakened his holiness? Maybe he can't turn water into Holy Water with the ease that Jesus turned water into wine?"

"Any way to test it?"

"I think Ben Bentley will be our test."

~ ~ ~

As was the habit since Marybelle Olsen came to manage the Hoople household, afternoon tea was served each day promptly at 3 p.m.

Tea is often seen as being inherently British. That's because the British East India Company had a monopoly over the tea industry for 60 years. Its consumption was encouraged by the British government because of the revenue it gained from taxing tea. As a result, tea became more popular than coffee, chocolate, and alcohol in England.

Today, Lady Greystone joined Maddy and her two aunts for "a cuppa." Tilly was usually there, always up for a tea party, but this particular afternoon had "taken to her bed." Beau usually avoided tea time, thinking it a "sissy" custom. Mark was at work, ensconced in his office at Town Hall. Madame Flora was "out and about." Aggie and N'yen (and Sissy) had their own agenda, as teenagers always do.

As today's tea, Marybelle Olsen had selected Tienchi, a very expensive brew cultivated from Panax Notoginseng flowers.

A Golden Needle

This sweet, minty tea is grown only once every three years in the Yunnan Province of China.

The history of tea goes back to 2737 BC when Emperor Shen Nung of China stirred a few leaves of the *Camellia sinensis* plant into a pot of boiling water and had the first-ever cup of tea.

"We want to ask you about your friend Cookie's husband, Ben Bentley," Aunt Hilda raised the question to Maddy.

"Yes, what about Ben?"

"Well, Helga and I have been thinking about what the ghost of Col. Madison told us about shooting that Count with a silver bullet. We've decided the man was a werewolf. Your husband won't discuss it with us, but there are many legends of werewolves here in Indiana."

Maddy shook her head, then took a sip of tea. "Dear, there's no such thing as a ghost. And there's no such thing as a werewolf either. You're letting Madame Flora get the best of your imaginations."

"Maybe not," said Helga. "There are stories we heard as children. Our mother – well we thought she was our mother – used to warn us to go to bed and stay there, else a werewolf would get us if he caught us wandering around the Mansion at night."

"Beau gets up and wanders the Mansion on many nights. A bad bladder. And he hasn't reported seeing any werewolves or ghosts or bogeymen."

"That's because he's descended from a long line of werewolf killers," nodded Aunt Hilda. "They fear him."

"Like that Van Helsing fellow who stalked Dracula," added Aunt Helga.

"You do know that Dracula was a fictional character invented by an Irish-born author named Bram Stoker?"

"Yes, but I've read that Dracula was based on a Romanian ruler known as Vlad the Impaler," whispered Aunt Hilda, as if imparting a secret.

"That's true," Maddy patted her arm. "But Vlad Țepeș was merely a cruel and bloodthirsty warlord, not a bloodsucking vampire."

"You say tomato, I say vampire," smiled Hilda. Unassailable in her mindset.

"Werewolves are real," asserted Helga. "I read a true story about one known as the Werewolf of Bedburg. Proof was the villagers cut off the wolf's paw and when they cornered it, the wolf turned into a man with his left hand missing."

"I know that story," replied Maddy. "A wealthy farmer named Peter Stumpp was accused of killing and devouring a number of children and women. Under severe torture, he confessed. But it's doubtful he was guilty. More likely he was convicted because he was a Protestant in a Catholic town. Politics, not lycanthropy."

"A Protestant can be a werewolf just as easily as anyone else," grumbled Helga. "Religion has nothing to do with the curse. It's non-denominational."

Maddy knew any argument was futile, so she gave up. "Now what were you saying about Ben Bentley?" she sighed.

"We think he's a werewolf."

Chapter Twenty

Made for Each Other

Heinrich and Florence were having one of their typical knock-down drag-out fights. This is why they could never stay married. But "business" kept bringing them back together. They were a good team when it came to running cons.

"You've gone too far this time," she was shouting at him, red in the face with rage. She was a good candidate for Anger Management School. They were in his seedy room at the Headliner Hotel. The walls were thin, but she didn't care who heard her. That was her incautious nature, loud and blowsy.

"I had to," he retorted. "We needed that journal with all the scribblings in the margins. And Robert Bob Roberts tried to hold me up on the price. I had no choice but kill him."

"That makes us murderers. We've never gone that far before. A short jail term for pulling a con is one thing; riding Ol' Sparky is another."

"Indiana has used lethal injection since 1995," he corrected her. "I looked it up. Indiana Code 35-38-6 requires that the execution by lethal injection take place inside the walls of the Indiana State Prison at Michigan City before sunrise."

"You idiot. Dead is dead, don't matter how they dispatch you. We've never put ourselves at risk like this before."

"A hazard of doing business. Robert Bob tried to hold us up. After I paid him five grand – quadruple the going price – but he wanted more. He asked for fifty percent of the action. No way I was gonna give him half a million dollars or more!"

"There's going to be plenty of money to go around. These Hooples are loaded. When they were kids their parents exhibited them like circus freaks – world famous quadruplets. They appeared before kings and presidents, princes and paupers. People paid to see them, paid them to appear in advertisements, paid them to sing and dance like trained monkeys."

Now Heinrich's face matched hers, as red as a ripe beefsteak tomato. "I know all that. I'm the one that does the research, in case you've forgotten. Turned out, them Hooples were a fraud. Their parents were pulling a con job just like us."

"But they didn't kill anybody. And those quadruplets got to keep all their money. They have a multimillion-dollar trust fund that's ripe for the plucking. That is, if we don't get arrested for murder."

"Nobody holds me up," he replied stubbornly. "Robert Bob Roberts crossed the line."

"He used to be a good resource for us, coming up with documents and papers that made our games seem legit. Now he's dead. Where will we get that kinda stuff now?"

"There are other autograph and rare manuscript dealers around. We will find one in Chicago."

"Yes, but they are likely to be honest. Robert Bob knew what we were up to. That's why he was so good at finding the right papers for each of our cons."

"He got too greedy. Now he's dead and gone. We'll find a replacement. Most of these autograph dealers are hinky, selling forged documents. I've heard about one in Chi-Town who also sells forged passports. We'll pick up a couple after this job in case we need to do a skip. We'll have enough dough to retire, spend the rest of our days on a beach in Belize or St. Barts."

"Together? I can't think of anything more depressing than spending the rest of our days together."

Heinrich laughed. "Like it or not, that's the way it's working out. None of our divorces have stuck."

"That's because we're in business together."

"No, it's because you're crazy about me. Ever since we were on stage together, we can't get enough of each other. Ain't no way you can quit me."

"We'll see about that. Men and women have separate prisons in Indiana."

~ ~ ~

Maddy and Aggie found Beau in the painting studio. A colorful palette balanced in one hand, a camelhair brush in the other, he was copying an impressionist landscape by William Forsythe. The oil painting showed a copse of trees with a dark river winding across the canvas. Forsyth was one of the five Indiana artists popularly known as the Hoosier Group. He was considered a "little cocky bantam rooster," but his paintings were masterpieces.

"I think I'm getting closer at matching Forsythe's brush strokes," he told them, proud of his progress. Rather than expressing his own innate creativity, painting was more of a therapeutic exercise for Beau. Doc Medford said it lowered his blood pressure.

"Very nice, dear," said his wife. An approving smile crossing her face.

"It's good to have the studio to myself today, without those two old bats yakking their nonsense in the background."

"Now, dear, be kind. We live here at the pleasure of Aunt Hilda and Aunt Helga. They mean well."

"I think they're getting more senile every day," Beau said. Glancing at his granddaughter, he added, "This is just between us grown-ups, right?" Recognizing that she was over 18 now.

"Okay, Grampy." Aggie paused, then continued, "I think they're getting weird too. They had me go online shopping for whistles that would scare away werewolves, if you can believe it."

"I do," nodded Maddy. "They told me they think Ben Bentley is a werewolf."

Beau chuckled. "Ben's hairy enough to be one," he said of his friend. "Back in high school we used to call him Cousin Itt – like that hair-covered character on *The Addams Family* TV show."

"But there's more to it," said Maddy. "This goes back to the séance where the spirit told everybody about Count Guicciardini being shot with a silver bullet. What's that all about, Pooh Bear? I know it has to do with the secrets passed down in your family from father to son. But I think it's about time to let the secret out in the open."

Her husband ducked his head, accepting the criticism. "You're right, dear. But most of the secret has been revealed – Col. Madison the First did kill the Count with a silver bullet."

"In a duel," Maddy encouraged his words.

"Not exactly. The Colonel shot the Count after the duel was over. Both discharged their flintlocks without hitting their target. Then, the Colonel stuffed his silver wedding ring into the barrel and fired again, this shot hitting the Count straight in the heart, killing him on the spot."

"But that would be murder," said Aggie. Shocked by the story about her distant ancestor – a revered Town Founder.

"True. But there were extenuating circumstances."

"Like what?" asked Maddy, doubtful.

"Count Guicciardini was a werewolf."

Chapter Twenty-One

Werewolves on the Run

"**H**ey, have you guys seen that old John Landis movie called *An American Werewolf in London*," asked N'yen. Lycanthropy being the topic of the day.

"What's it about?" asked Sissy. They were hanging out in the game room, playing Clabber, a four-player trick-taking card game that's native to Indiana.

"The movie's about two American backpackers who are attacked by a werewolf on the British moors. One dies and the other turns into a werewolf during a full moon."

"Yes, I know that movie," said Aggie. "I though David Naughton was dreamy in it. I love that scene of him rampaging around Piccadilly Circus as a snarling wolf. Way cool."

"Werewolves roaming about London, hey?" chimed in Leslie Ann. "Therianthropy – or animal transformation – is a recurrent theme in British folklore. Reminds me of that old Welsh poem '*Pa Gwr yw y Porthwr*.' Traced back to 1250, it tells about the *Gwrgi Garwlwyd* – that translates as 'Man Dog Rough Grey' – a monster who killed a Briton each day, with two on Saturday so he could rest on Sunday. He was no doubt a werewolf."

"That's a very obscure reference," said Aggie.

"Not if you're British."

"I rest my case," smiled Aggie.

"Want something closer to home? Then you oughta like this song called 'Werewolves of Indiana,'" said N'yen, pressing the PLAY on his iPhone screen.

The music was bouncy, a tune by Mother of Earl:

"You say I couldn't get much worse
But I just blame this ancient curse
While Indiana it may burn
A man can change, a man can learn
So take your hand off of the gun
We're just werewolves on the run."

"Not bad, but I prefer 'Bark at the Moon' by Ozzy Osbourne," said Aggie.

Sissy replied, "I like 'Witch Wolf' by STYX." She began to sing:

"Reoccurring symptoms
Answer the baleful howl
Bringing me dreams of darkness
The doer of all that's foul"

She had a pitch-perfect singing voice.

"Nice, but I think Warren Zevon does it best with 'Werewolves of London," said Leslie Ann. "It has drums by Mick Fleetwood and electric bass by John McVie. You can't get much better than that."

"Can't argue with that," said N'yen.

"And don't you just love that refrain," she added. Starting to howl:

"Aaoooooo!
Werewolves of London ...
Aaoooooo!"

"You know, you're pretty cool for a countess," smiled Aggie.

"And you're pretty cool for a commoner," laughed Leslie Ann.

Chapter Twenty-Two

Who's There?

Knock! Knock!

Cookie Bentley opened the front door of the farmhouse and smiled when she saw her visitors. "Hilda, Helga, so good to see you. To what do we owe this pleasure? You ladies don't get out very much."

"Oh, we're getting around more and more as of late," responded Hilda. "I've taken up driving again."

"She's a regular Mario Andretti," nodded her sister. "She nearly hit 35 MPH coming up Highway 21 on the way here."

"Impressive," said Cookie. She knew neither sister had a driver's license. She'd better call Maddy to report her aunts' illegal activities. Someone could get hurt with Hilda's weaving all over the road. "Won't you come in for some watermelon tea? I've made a fresh pitcher."

"No, thank you. We came to see your husband. Brought him this, uh, lemonade." Hilda held up a Mason jar filled with a colorless liquid.

"Oh, how thoughtful of you," Cookie said. "Ben, come out here. Hilda and Helga brought you something."

"Oh, hi," Ben Bentley said as he filled the doorway, a broad grin on his face. "Wanna say we had a great time at your garden party. It was a nice event."

No sooner had he spoken than Hilda Hoople splashed the contents of the Mason jar into his face. "Evil, be gone!" she shouted.

Her sister added, "Amen."

"What the –?" gulped Cookie's surprised husband.

115

"Hilda, what are you doing?" shouted Cookie, wiping Ben's face with the dishcloth in her hands.

"I'm okay," he said. "Just startled me."

"Hilda, Helga, what was that all about?" Cookie turned to confront the elderly women on her doorstep. But by the time she said these words, the attackers were already in their old Rolls Royce, grinding it to life, making their escape like Bonnie and ... Bonnie.

Cookie and Ben watched in baffled silence as the two women drove away.

~ ~ ~

Sissy's grandfather – Buck Jackson, Beau's old Army buddy – was out for his afternoon constitutional. When his gout wasn't flaring up, he tried to get in a good five-mile hike at least once a week. An old military habit. He usually followed a trail that led up past Bottomless Sinkhole toward Injun Woods.

Funny how it was called "Bottomless" when you could see the brick chimney of the house it swallowed sticking up above the muddy surface of the water. Just past the sinkhole was Injun Woods. That was the forested campground used by the Son of Anthony Wayne, the statewide camper organization headed by Cookie Bentley's husband, Ben.

On the way back, Buck was surprised to see a car turning into the dead-end road that led up to a shack known as Helga's Hideaway. This was the spot Maddy Madison's ersatz Aunt Helga had hidden out when people thought she was dead, a suicide in the geyser at Gruesome Gorge State Park. But turns out, she was pulling a Greta Garbo, just wanting to be alone.

"Now that's odd," Buck said to himself. "Who's going up to that abandoned shack?" He had a habit of talking out loud to himself. And sometimes answering. Some people thought it was a sign of oncoming dementia; others merely considered his one-way conversations as eccentric.

Out of curiosity, Buck turned up the rutted road, walking in the direction of the out-of-place automobile. "Do you think it's kids going up there to make out?" he asked himself. He was worried that his granddaughter had just turned Sweet Sixteen and was showing interest in boys – particularly that little Vietnamese boy. Buck wasn't sure how he felt about that. He'd fought Gooks in 'Nam. He'd spent over ten I-love-the-smell-of-napalm-in-the-morning years in the jungles of that faraway land.

"No, not kids," he answered himself. "That looked like two older folks in that rusty Buick Lacrosse."

"Maybe it could be burglars, breaking into Helga Hoople's old house," he posited. "Doubt there's anything valuable left up there."

"Well, you best be a good citizen and go check," he told himself. "Them old Hoople gals have been mighty good to you, having you and Sissy over to dinner any number of times."

He hiked up the dirt road, trying to keep his voice down so he wouldn't be heard coming. He'd had reconnaissance training in the military. He'd avoided Charlie snipers in 'Nam by keeping his mouth closed when on patrols into Indian Country. And he followed that same protocol now, zipping his lip, moving stealthily up the road, approaching the house carefully, keeping his eyes on the aeruginous blue car parked in front of the squat little building.

He could hear a conversation emanating from inside Helga's Hideaway. The woman's voice was loud, a shouter. "You can stay here. It's a lot cheaper than that Headliner Hotel down in Burpyville."

The answer was unintelligible.

"You may as well get used to it. This deal is gonna take longer than we thought. We wanna go for the big bucks, we gotta get the hook in deep. Are you with me on this, Heinie?"

Another unintelligible response.

"Then it's decided. Take me back to the Mansion and I'll let you know when I need another visit from Col. Madison."

Buck stepped behind an oak tree as the car reversed its way down the narrow dirt road, heading back toward town. He didn't recognize the weaselly bald-headed guy driving the car, but the passenger was none other than that medium staying at the Hoople Mansion – what was her name? – oh yeah, Madame Florida or something like that.

What was she doing up here at Helga's Hideaway? The place was supposed to be abandoned.

Should he report this to the police? No, the woman was a guest in the Hoople Mansion. Maybe she had permission to be here.

Nonetheless, he'd have to mention this sighting to his ol' pal Beau Madison. "Yes, you do that," he said to himself out loud, now that he was alone. "That pair looked like they were up to no good. Can't have that."

Chapter Twenty-Three

That Jacob Caruthers Journal

Police Chief Jim Purdue – Bootsie's husband – had been turning a blind eye to Madame Flora up 'til now. Although the town of Caruthers Corners had anti-fortune-telling laws on the books, they were not strenuously enforced. Mainly, because there were not many instances of commercial mediums, psychics, and tarot card readers in this part of northeastern Indiana.

A few years ago, they had dealt with a psychic who promised to exorcize the ghost in Beasley Manor, but the invasive spirit turned out to be a low-level crook hiding out in the abandoned building.

The police chief worried that Madame Flora was some sort of scam artist, but the fact remained she was the guest of Tilly Tidemore, wife of the town's mayor. So it wasn't in Jim's best interest to harass the interloper.

Apparently, Madame Flora was clairvoyant enough to realize her impunity. The woman came and went as if she were a famous movie star. She even stopped on the street to sign autographs when asked. She had a certain over-the-top look about her, like a Gypsy Romani.

She reminded him of a Spanish ballad he'd once heard:

"There meets her a Gypsy
So fluent of talk,
And jauntily dressed,
On the principal walk."

However, that afternoon things changed. Mark Tidemore shared with Jim the report of a private investigator he'd hired to look into Madame Flora. No surprise that she and her sometimes husband had a long list of infractions as scammers. What was a surprise is that Mark the Shark asked him not to act on this information, but instead keep an eye on the situation.

Mark had invited his father-in-law to join them for this confab in his second-floor office at the Town Hall. Time to put their heads together on this Madame Flora business.

Beau was way ahead of them in suspecting Madame Flora of being a fraud. No way the ghost of his long-dead great-grandfather was bringing him messages from the Great Beyond. Like his wife, Beau was a level-headed, sober-minded skeptic when it came to séances and mediums and talking spirit guides. He was religious but not crazy. That is, if you could discount this werewolf business.

At the meeting, Beau had one additional piece of information to share: His old army buddy Buck Jackson had spotted Madame Flora and a bullet-headed man with a moustache poking around Helga's Hideaway up near Bottomless Sinkhole.

Mark figured the unknown man might be Florence Bashinski's estranged husband Heinrich. His private eye said they often worked confidence games together.

Jim hadn't seen any sign of Heinrich Bashinski around town, but said he'd assign one of his deputies to check out the abandoned shack where Madame Flora and the man had been spotted by Buck Jackson. A charge of criminal trespass might take Madame Flora's confederate out of the game.

"Wait till in the morning," advised Beau. "Let's hear what this Heinrich guy has to say at the séance tonight, assuming he's the voice of Col. Beauregard Madison. I want to figure out how the 'ghost' knew about my great-grandfather's silver bullet. That's not in any of the history books."

"Okay with you?" the mayor asked his police chief.

Jim Purdue nodded reluctantly. "First thing in the morning then." Beau Madison was his best friend, so he went along with the request ... even if it was against his better judgement. "But here's the thing, I want you to wear a wire to the séance tonight. Okay?"

"Sure, no problem. You'll get a kick out of this charade. My great-grandfather is sure to make an appearance."

Nobody had any doubt that Madame Flora and her confederate had their greedy eyes on the Hoople Quadruple millions – a plum target for any grifter looking for a get-rich-quick shortcut to the Good Life. However, Chief Jim Purdue had a different kind of Good Life in mind for this duplicitous duo, one that involved free room and board in the state's penitentiary system.

~ ~ ~

"One other thing," said Beau. "The so-called spirit said there had been *two* deaths. The first was my great-grandfather killing that Count. We know this to be a historical fact. But he said there had been another death connected to the quilt just a week or so ago."

"Nobody's died here in the last several weeks," Jim Purdue assured him. "At least not a violent death."

"You sure?" asked the Mayor.

"Hang on and I'll have my deputy run a quick search. Tommy's a whiz on the computer."

Beau nodded. "Yes, I hear he and my grandson are fierce online gaming competitors."

"That's what Tommy says. Just give me a few minutes to have him check on this."

Ten minutes later, Tommy Truehart called back.

Mark and his father-in-law could only hear Chief Purdue's side of the conversation:

"Yes … yes … yes … okay … thanks." He was writing on a yellow legal pad as he talked. That is, if "Yes … yes … yes … okay … thanks" was considered talk.

"Well?" said Beau when the Chief put the phone down.

Jim Purdue ran his hand over his slick scalp, a gesture that mirrored his puzzlement. "Don't see anything," he said. "Tommy checked with Yost and Yost. The funeral home hasn't had a single customer in two weeks. Not even a heart attack or a jaywalker stepping in front of a truck. They were complaining about business being slow."

"I had the impression the spirit was talking about a violent death," said Beau.

"Yes, Tommy checked that too. Over in Burpyville, there was a classroom shooting – you heard about that on TV – and a victim of domestic violence. And a fatal traffic accident. None sounds like it fits the bill."

"No, it doesn't."

"Down in Indy, they had their usual share of violent crimes," he said, consulting his notes. "A convenience store hold-up. A head-on collision. A slip-and-fall. Several COVID deaths, but I suppose you'd call that natural causes."

"Nothing there."

"Oh, there was a burglary than didn't go well. The proprietor of an autograph shop got shot during a break-in."

"Autographs?"

"Yeah, a place called – let me see where I wrote it down – Robert's Rare Hoosier-Only Autographs & Manuscripts. That couldn't be connected could it?"

"Rare manuscripts … that sounds like a possibility."

"I'll have Tommy get more details."

~ ~ ~

"Bingo!" said Chief Purdue. The Indy police had just confirmed that the cash register records at Robert's Rare Hoosier-Only Autographs & Manuscripts Emporium showed the last two items the shop sold: One was an undelivered letter from a Count Antonio Guicciardini. The second was an annotated copy of a book called *My Journey into Indian Territory, 1829.*

The letter was a clear connection to Madame Flora's otherworldly hokum. The so-called spirit had spoken of a Count Guicciardini.

The book was more puzzling. Bo had just left, so Jim Purdue picked up the phone and called the Caruthers Corners Public Library.

Dorothy Starcatcher answered. As the town's new librarian, she was busy stocking shelves. The 2018 tornado had completely destroyed the old library, books and all. But now that the library had moved into one of the wings of the Perricock Museum, things seemed to be returning to normal. A grant from Maddy Madison's small foundation was paying for new books.

"Hello," said the voice of Dorothy Starcatcher.

Chief Purdue failed to respond. It suddenly occurred to him that the librarian was part of Tilly Tidemore's séance group. It might be risky to ask her about a rare book that might connect Madame Flora – or her husband – to a murder.

He quietly hung up. And called the Caruthers Corners Historical Society, located in a wing of the museum maybe 50 steps from the doors to the new library.

Cookie Bentley had no trouble identifying the book in question. "*My Journey into Indian Territory, 1829* – that's the name of the journal kept by Jacob Caruthers, one of the Town Founders," she said confidently, as if giving a winning answer in a trivia contest.

"Everybody knows who Jacob Caruthers is," Chief Purdue responded irritably. "The town's named after the old scallywag. I just didn't know the name of his book."

"We have the original journal here at the Historical Society. That must be one from the published edition. It was a vanity project of former mayor Henry Caruthers. An attempt to aggrandize his ancestor. It was a very small print run, maybe two thousand copies. That makes the book fairly rare."

"Is there anything in there about Count Guicciardini? Or his duel with Col. Madison?"

Cookie called on her HSAM ability. The pages of *My Journey into Indian Territory, 1829* flew past her mind's eye like images on a Microfiche machine. "A brief mention of the duel. Nothing about a silver bullet. The Count isn't identified by name."

"Shucks."

"What's your interest in the Caruthers journal?"

"An annotated copy was stolen. I think it's somehow linked to Madame Flora."

"Annotated?"

"That's what the Indy police report said. What's that mean exactly?

"Annotated means there are comments in the margins, explaining or expounding on something in the adjacent text. There are all kind of annotated books. *The Annotated Wizard of Oz. The Annotated Gulliver's Travels. The Annotated Shakespeare.*"

"And an *Annotated My Journey into Indian Territory, 1829?*"

"I've never heard of one."

"That's strange. Looks like a rare manuscript dealer was killed by someone who wanted to get his hands on it."

~ ~ ~

The Indy police were closing in on Heinrich Bashinski. Robert's Rare Hoosier-Only Autographs & Manuscripts Emporium had a video surveillance system, the camera hidden in a book on a top shelf, the recorder in a closet in the back room. The tape had a grainy image of Heinrich shooting the autograph dealer. Robert Bob Roberts had used and reused the old-fashioned video tape till it was as blurry as a smeared image in a newspaper left in the rain. But they were able to make out the visage of a short, bald man – a match for a petty criminal known as Heinrich Anatol Bashinski A/K/A Henry Aaron Bascom A/K/A Hank Bennett.

The detectives on the case had traced Heinrich Bashinski to the Highliner Hotel in Burpyville. But the perp had checked out just the day before, no forwarding address. He had to still be in the area, they told themselves.

Chapter Twenty-Four
The Quilt's Rightful Owner

Cookie Bentley had the first success. In the basement of the Caruthers Corners Town Hall where all the property records, deeds, liens, marriage certificates, and such were stored, she and Bootsie came across a handwritten death certificate for one Antonio Francesco Guicciardini.

> Date and Time of Death: 7:45 a.m., June 12, 1832.
>
> Cause of Death: Gunshot wound to the heart. Killed following a duel with Col. Beauregard Madison.
>
> Notation: Witnesses say both shots missed, then Guicciardini rushed the Col. screaming and foaming at the mouth. The Col. hurriedly fired a second shot, stopping his opponent in his tracks.

Hmm, that was interesting. While Cookie had seen the record of death in the town's fledgling computerized database, she had never seen the actual document before. That notation about a shot following the duel was worth noting.

~ ~ ~

Lady Greystone was the next to turn up something. She came up with the idea of checking for any Guicciardinis in San Francisco. See if they knew anything about the family quilts.

A quick Google search located a Jonathan M. Guicciardini, MD. His medical clinic had a website that listed a phone number. Dr. Guicciardini specialized in plastic surgery. The website sported a slogan: The Italian Way to Beauty Is Only a Nip and Tuck Away.

The doctor came on the line, saying, "My receptionist says you're calling about the Tristan and Iseult Quilt. My family sold that off in 1927."

"So I understand. But I'm told they held onto a piece of the quilt for themselves."

"And what if they did?"

"I'm told that a relative shipped it to one of your ancestors back in the 1800s."

"According to family tradition, they sent it by courier but it never arrived. Some cousin ran away with the quilt fragment. It has never turned up. Probably wound up in some private collection."

"I appreciate you taking the time to speak with me."

"You sound pretty nice, that British accent and all. If you ever need a little augmentation -- say, make your boobs perky again – just let me know."

"Thanks, but my boobs are quite perky," Leslie Ann said. "At least my husband thinks so."

Dr. Guicciardini chuckled. "I like your spunk," he said. "If I can ever help you with that quilt business, let me know. Or if those perky boobs ever need an uplift."

"I'll keep that in mind," Leslie Ann said as she hung up.

~ ~ ~

"Got it all figured out," N'yen announced. "Where ol' Antonio stashed the quilt."

"Oh?" said his grandmother.

"Yep. I just applied a little logic. He wouldn't have buried it in the ground or stuck it in a hollow tree. It would have rotted or mildewed. And he wouldn't have had access to private places like the Caruthers Mansion or other early structures."

"So where then?"

"He gave it to a friend to hold for him."

"But any friend would be long gone. That was nearly two centuries ago."

"The families are still around. Maybe it's stashed away in somebody's attic."

"But whose?"

"Maybe the person whose wagon he was a passenger on."

~ ~ ~

Cookie went through the wagon train's manifest in her head. All the names were known, but it wasn't clear who shared the same wagons.

"It was a long train," Maddy noted. "Close to twenty Conestoga wagons, each pulled by a team of eight horses. Close to eighty settlers in all. And one of them was Count Antonio Guicciardini on his way to San Francisco."

"Yes, Dr. Jonathan Guicciardini confirmed the family history that a cousin was bringing them a piece of the Tristan Quilt," nodded Leslie Ann.

"But he never showed up," Aggie completed the story.

"Maybe he stole it," suggested Sissy.

"That's what the family thinks," confirmed the Countess.

"But he died here in a duel," Bootsie pointed out. "So the quilt should still be around here somewhere."

"No, he died after the duel was over," Cookie corrected her. "But you're right, it should still be somewhere around here."

"But where?" said Maddy.

"I think he would have left it with a friend," insisted N'yen. "Makes sense."

"Who did he know?" puzzled Lizzie.

"Like I said, someone he befriended on the wagon train," argued the boy.

"But who?" said his grandmother.

"Whose wagon was he on?" asked Aggie.

"Yes, likely he bonded with his wagon mate on the perilous journey to Indiana," agreed Leslie Ann. "That's the party for whom we should be looking."

"I've got it narrowed down," Cookie said. "The Count had to have been on one of three wagons – Tom Bodkins, Archie Aitkens, or Hezekiah Taylor. All the rest were families or related travelers."

Maddy perked up. "Hezekiah Taylor was one of my ancestors, the brother of Rev. Thaddeus Taylor, my great-grandfather." Maddy's maiden name had been Taylor. Before she discovered she was a Hoople.

Lizzie said, "If Hezekiah Taylor was the Count's travel pal, does the Taylor family have the quilt?"

"Not that I know of. There was just that quilt made by Rev. Thaddeus Taylor's wife. And one made by great-aunt Sally, but it was a mess so my mother packed it away. Aunt Sally wasn't very adept at sewing."

"I always heard that Hezekiah Taylor was a saloonkeeper," commented Lizzie, fluffing her read hair absently.

"A minister's brother?"

"Sadly so. He was the Black Sheep of the family."

Being the resident historian, Cookie spoke up: "Taylor's Tavern, for years it was the only saloon in town," she affirmed. "And there hasn't been a bar here since it closed down in 1865 when ol' Hezekiah joined the 22nd Independent Infantry Regiment. According to the records, he was killed in the Battle of Perryville, Kentucky, where his regiment suffered a 65 percent casualty rate. That was one of the highest losses in a single engagement by any regiment during the entire Civil War."

"Sounds like he made a pretty poor soldier, losing that badly," observed Aggie.

"Maybe because he drank too much. It was said he had a 'hollow leg' when it came to whiskey," said Maddy.

"But no quilt?" pressed Lizzie.

"Not as far as I know."

"Okay, what about this Tom Bodkins?" asked Bootsie. "I don't know anybody hereabouts named Bodkins."

Cookie had the answer there too. "Tom Bodkins was a bachelor, never married. The line died out with him."

"If the Count entrusted the quilt with Tom Bodkins, who would *he* have passed it to?" asked Leslie Ann, trying to follow the thread.

"Beats me," said Cookie. "I can follow the genealogy charts, but that doesn't tell me who their friends were."

"That leaves – what was his name?" continued Leslie Ann.

"Aitkens, Archie Aitkens," Cookie supplied the name.

"Any relation to Floyd Aitkens or his daughter Susy Q?" asked Maddy. Aitkens Produce was the largest watermelon farm in the county. After Floyd died, his daughter turned the farm over to the town to run as a co-op.

"You guessed it," nodded Cookie. "Floyd was a direct descendent of one Archibald Reginald Aitkens."

"I suppose we could talk with Susy Q," said Bootsie. Ol' Floyd got blown to Kingdom Come in a meth lab explosion. His daughter Susan had married Chief Purdue's former deputy Petie Hitzer and now helped him run the family dairy farm.

"And I can look through the trunk that my mother – uh, adopted mother – left me, see if there's anything in there of interest besides Aunt Sally's Picasso Patchwork."

"Picasso Patchwork?" said Aggie. Her interest perked up, knowing she was likely to be the heir to the hodgepodge of quilts and coverlets and embroideries that filled that big leather trunk in the storage room at the Mansion.

"That sounds valuable," said Sissy. Even in Alabama, folks had heard of the famous Spanish artist known for his Cubism paintings.

"Not really," laughed Maddy. "We merely called Aunt Sally's portrait quilt that because the images on it were all out of kilter. Eyes out of place, noses on crooked."

"Maybe it was an accurate depiction of some of the Crackletons," joked Aggie. "They're pretty weird." Those strange people who lived up in Crackleton Crossing were known for their deformities – one guy (a victim of the vanishing twin syndrome) even had three eyes.

"Hush," Maddy playfully swiped at her granddaughter. "Don't forget that you're related to the Crackletons. Technically, Granny Crackleton is your great-great-grandmother."

"Yes, I know. Is it possible to get a gene transplant?"

"Thank goodness I'm adopted," said N'yen. It wasn't clear whether he was joking or not.

Maddy merely shook her head.

"Is Granny Crackleton really a witch?" asked Sissy, who believed in such oddball superstitions.

"Ain't no such thing," scoffed N'yen – Mr. Science!

"Is too," retorted Sissy. "One lived down the block from us in Birmingham. She could turn you into a frog."

"That's silly," N'yen rolled his eyes.

"Hey, this is the land of religious freedom," said Sissy. "Aggie's a Baptist, you're a Buddhist, and I can believe in witches if I wanna."

"Okay, okay. But don't go casting any spells on me."

Aggie started singing:

"She looked at my palm and she made a magic sign,
She said 'What you need is Love Potion Number Nine.'"

"Cut that out," said her cousin.

She just grinned, knowing she'd scored a bulls-eye.

"Okay, let's get going on our quests," said Lizzie, bringing them back to the subject at hand. "Bootsie and I will go talk to Susy Q. Maddy, you and your brood check out the Taylor hand-me-downs. Cookie, you and Leslie Ann keep digging into the town history, looking for where the Count might have lived or who his friends might have been."

"Aye, aye," said Aggie. Laughing at her Aunt Lizzie's take-charge demeanor. She had just regrouped the teams.

"Don't you mock me, young lady. Else I won't help you finish that Easy Street quilt that has you stuck."

"Yes, ma'am." Despite its name, the Easy Street was a difficult quilt because of its 1,500 or so pieces.

"I have another idea," interrupted N'yen. Snapping his fingers as if turning on a switch inside his head.

"What is it?" asked Lizzie. The redhead's attention shifting from Aggie to the girl's genius cousin. Perhaps she had a touch of "Look, there's a squirrel" ADHD.

N'yen offered a broad smile. "What if we simply ask the ghost of Col. Madison where to find the quilt?"

Chapter Twenty-Five

Behold a False Prophet

T he idea of N'yen Madison – the no-nonsense, scientific-minded, anti-superstition, reason-and-logic brainiac who was majoring in astrophysics at Northwestern – suggesting that they should consult a ghost was mind-bogging to the members of the Quilters Club.

"Beg pardon?" said Lizzie, thinking she had not heard him right.

"Have you lost your marbles?" blurted Aggie, staring at him as if he had been taken over by Pod People.

"You're suggesting we go to a séance?" his grandmother tried to clarify the statement.

"Ask Col. Madison?" Cookie repeated his words, as if considering the suggestion.

"An interesting proposal," mused the Lady Greystone.

"I think it's a super-duper idea," said Sissy, being supportive of her prospective boyfriend. Despite their quasi-quarrel about witches.

N'yen smiled slyly. "I don't mean for real. But that fake ghost knew about the silver bullet and the duel and the Tristan Quilt. So Madame Flora may know even more if we can get her talking."

~ ~ ~

Madame Flora wore a billowy yellow dress with plenty of petticoats, a white blouse with puffy sleeves, and a multicolored knit shawl, an outfit that gave her a gypsy-like appearance, in keeping with her role as a fortune teller.

But the main purpose of the yards of cotton and silk was to hide her paraphernalia. To carry out her "performance," she relied on a filtered laser pointer, a nut-sized transmitter, an itsy bitsy speaker, and an aerosol spray strapped to her ankle that created a fine mist she passed off as ectoplasm. Tools of her trade, she called them.

Perhaps not all mediums were deliberate charlatans, spiritualism being a religious choice. Nonetheless – as debunkers like Harry Houdini and The Amazing Randi found – it was fertile ground for fraud. Being a soothsayer or prognosticator or oracle was one of Florence Bashinski's favorite scams. She had once dreamed of becoming an actress, and this was as close as one could come to thespianism without actually being on stage or screen.

Some people – like that movie star Shirley MacLaine – actually believed in past lives and channeling spirits. Others people believed in Jesus. And still others believed in UFOs. To each his own, Florence told herself.

The modified laser was used to create the glow near the ceiling that she identified as her spirit guide, Arthur Conan Doyle. The transmitter picked up Heinrich's voice broadcasting from nearby, passing himself off as Doyle or someone's Uncle Fred ... or Col. Beauregard Madison.

Heinrich was a pretty good actor himself. That's where he met Florence, in a Little Theater production of *Guys and Dolls*. He'd played Nathan Detroit; she was Miss Adelaide. He liked to think he could have had a Hollywood career if things had broken the right way. But life was disappointing.

These days he enjoyed his roles as spirits. He was particularly good at doing voices, he thought. At this distance, transmission was clear as a bell. Florence's – that is, Madame Flora's – layered skirt muffled the sound enough to give it an eerie otherworldly quality. You'd think he was right there in the room.

Tonight, another séance was scheduled. In addition to Tilly Tidemore, that librarian and the other woman, plus the two aunts, both Beau Madison and his wife Maddy would be in attendance. Madame Flora has specifically invited them, promising more revelations about the missing quilt fragment.

Getting the hook in.

That's why an appearance was scheduled for ol' Beauregard Madison the First. This would be the one where the spirit asked them to put up "good faith" money for the location of the Tristan Quilt.

Not that Henrich had any idea where to find the quilt. Or even if there actually was such a quilt. All that was important was that the marks believed in it.

Chapter Twenty-Six
The Séance

The séance began promptly at midnight. An optimum time to receive spirit visits, explained Madame Flora. The Gateway between Life and Death is a thinner membrane at that hour, she said.

Aunt Hilda and Aunt Helga were dressed in their finery. You would have thought they were going to an Easter Parade. Madame Flora asked them to remove their hats, providing better "connectivity" with the Spirit World.

Maddy and Beau had been invited to sit in, what with Beau expecting a further message from his roughshod antecedent, Col. Beauregard Hollingsworth Madison the First.

Tilly looked dreamy-eyed, as if she was hopped up on Librium or a similar tranquilizer. Mark sat beside her in a $2,000 suit that made him look like a big-city lawyer ready to face the Supreme Court.

Dorothy Stargazer was there, but Faith Ann Crackleton was not. Word was, Faith Ann had broken her big toe, dropping a case of Campbell's Tomato Soup on it while stocking shelves at her family's convenience store up at the Crossing.

Lady Greystone had been invited, but declined. She had her standing as British royalty to consider. The tabloids would have a ball with a story of her attending a séance.

Aggie, being 18, had been eligible to attend, but she reluctantly declined because N'yen and Sissy, both 16, had been excluded. "Age discrimination," N'yen had muttered grumpily.

"I would have paid a nickel to be a fly on the wall for that séance," Aggie told them. Regretting her noble decision to stick with her friends.

"Okay, pay me the five cents," said N'yen, holding out his olive hand, palm-up.

"What for?"

"Because I have a directional microphone. I think it will pick up conversations next door." The cupola where they sat was less than twenty feet from the twin cupola where the séance was taking place.

"You sure?" said Sissy. Her grandfather had agreed that she could spend the night with her friend Aggie. "These stone walls are ten feet thick."

"Closer to two feet," Aggie corrected her exaggeration.

There was a knock at the door and Leslie Ann appeared. "I thought you young detectives might have figured out a way to eavesdrop," she said accusingly. Then winked and added, "May join you?"

"Sure thing," beckoned Aggie, scooting over to make room on the comfortable day bed. Other than this plush sanctuary, N'yen Madison's room looked like a Mad Scientist's laboratory, crowded with gizmos and electronic devices and telescopes.

Sissy grinned. "Hey there, Lady Grey– uh, Leslie Ann. You got here just in time. N'yen's tuning up his directional microphone."

Leslie Ann glanced at the device. "Will it work with these thick walls?"

"That's what I just said," Sissy replied.

"Hang on, I'll show you," the boy said as he fiddled with dials. There was a sound like a radio station with a poor signal. Then the voices became clearer. "Got it," he nodded, locking in on the exact wavelength.

"Arthur Conan Doyle, are you there?" came Madame Flora's distant voice. The séance had already started.

Silence.

"Arthur Conan Doyle, are you there?" Madame Flora repeated.

There was a bit more static, then a deeper voice replied, "I am right 'ere, luv."

"Tonight we want to reach Col. Beauregard Hollingsworth Madison, the ancestor of one of our guests. Can you locate him?"

"Toodleydoo, the Colonel's standing 'ere next to me," came the ersatz British voice. "Ready to weep and wail."

"That's a phony accent," frowned Leslie Ann. "Arthur Ignatius Conan Doyle was actually born in Scotland. He was sent to school in England at nine. From there, he went to school in Austria where he studied German. Then for the next five years he studied medicine in Edinburgh. He certainly didn't speak with a Cockney accent."

"I knew it was fake," said Aggie.

"What's Cockney?" asked Sissy.

"A dialect spoken by working-class East Londoners," Leslie Ann explained. "They replace the 'th' sound in words such as 'think' with an F sound. Likewise, the 'H' sound in words such as 'holiday' will be dropped entirely, so that the words are instead pronounced as 'oliday.' They also use rhyming slang, where everything rhymes with what it actually means. 'China plate' means 'mate.' It's very complicated."

"That's nothing," Sissy gave a dismissing wave of her hand. "You should try talking jive."

"I'm getting interference with my signal," griped N'yen. "I think that ghost's voice is actually a radio transmission."

"Where from?" asked Sissy, looking around the room as if the culprit might be among them.

"Dunno," said the boy. "Look out the window and see if you spot anybody. Nobody could get inside the Mansion. It's locked up for the night. But this is probably coming from someplace nearby."

Aggie pressed her face against a window, her breath fogging the glass. "Nobody's in front of the Mansion," she said. "Oh wait, there's a car parked over at the museum. Could it be coming from there?"

"I'd bet a nickel it is."

"Hey, that's my nickel you're betting," said Aggie.

"Hush, there's another voice."

"Greetings from the Great Beyond," a rougher voice was saying over the speaker. "I want to speak to Beauregard the Fourth."

~ ~ ~

"Is that you, great-grandpa?" answered Beau. Trying to sound serious.

"Yes, it is me, laddie, the founder of the Madison lineage," came a tinny voice. "But I am here in spirit only. I cannot exude enough ectoplasm to form a corporal vision of myself. You may only see a faint glow of me until I build up more power."

"Is that you up near the ceiling? Right near where Arthur Conan Doyle was floating?"

"Yes. You can see my glow emanating through the portal between here and the Other Side."

"Colonel, I wanted to ask you about the silver bullet you shot Count Guicciardini with. Where did you get it?"

"Get what?"

"That silver bullet. I don't expect you normally carried one in your cartridge belt."

"Oh, uh, no, of course not. It was given to me as a gift by a fearless vampire hunter named Bram Stoker. Told me to take it with me to the duel. Said I might need it."

Beau knew that was a lie. The "bullet" had been Col. Madison's wedding ring. That's why the lump of silver was passed down through the generations. And Bram Stoker – what a hoot!

"Are you sure about that?" Beau replied. "Bram Stoker was the writer who penned that fictional book about *Dracula*. But Stoker wasn't born until about fifteen years *after* your duel with Count Guicciardini."

"I am sure you are mistaken, grandson. I knew him well. A glum sort of fellow. He was passing through on a speaking tour."

"I'm pretty sure Bram Stoker never visited this part of Indiana."

"Uh, it was a secret side trip. When he wasn't writing scary stories he was gallivanting around the country with other writers – like that guy who wrote *Frankenstein*."

"A woman wrote *Frankenstein*."

"That's what I meant."

"With all due respect, I've read Bram Stoker's *Dracula*, Mary Shelly's *Frankenstein*. Even Sabine Baring-Gould's *The Book of Werewolves*. I'm pretty sure they didn't know each other. Stoker was four years old when Mary Shelly died."

"Never mind that, laddie. I bring you secrets from Beyond the Grave. Do you want to know where to find the priceless Tristan Quilt? It's worth a huge fortune. And it's just waiting for you to claim it."

Beau hesitated, then continued as planned. "Yes, tell me about the quilt."

"The Tristan Quilt is in the hands of a man named Luigi Guicciardini, a great-grandson of the Count. He does not know the true value of the quilt. He will sell it to you for one million dollars cash. Then you can sell it to the Bargello Museum for fifty million."

"How do I find this Luigi character?"

143

"Tomorrow at noon he will be having lunch at that silver-fronted diner in town. You can find him there. He will have the quilt fragment in the trunk of his car, a Buick Lacrosse. Bring the money with you – $1-million in $100 bills."

"How does he know to come there?"

"Because I've already brokered the deal for you. I appeared to Luigi in a dream and told him you'd be there with the money.

Beau didn't bother telling him there was no way to gather $1-million in cash by noon tomorrow. Banks didn't keep that much cash lying around waiting for an on-the-spot withdrawal. Certainly not a small institution like Caruthers Corners Savings & Loan. Besides, he had no intention of paying any of the money. But he said, "Good, I will be there at noon with the cash."

"I now return the control to Mr. Conan Doyle. He can find me if you need my help again."

There was a moment of silent. Then a voice that said, "Cheerio, I 'ope you'll take the Colonel's advice. Bring the bees and honey. That quilt's one of a kind."

"I thought there were two other pieces," muttered Beau.

"Whatever you say, guv'nor. Three of a kind. I'm signing off now. See you next time, Madame Flora. Laters."

"Oooo," said the medium, as if coming out of a trance. "Where am I? Oh yes, I'm here in the Hoople Mansion with my good friend Tilly. Were the spirits helpful?"

Chapter Twenty-Seven
Taking the Photograph

Aggie and Sissy circled the parked Buick, keeping low so the driver wouldn't see them. They were breathing hard, having run down Hoople Hill and trudged up High Jinks Hill on the asphalt road that led to the museum. Whew, that was quite a climb!

Clouds blanketed the nighttime sky. Darkness surrounded them like an invisibility cloak. There was no moon. Aggie busied herself at the rear of the car, punching an ice pick into one of the rear wheels. "That oughta hold him," she whispered to her friend. "That tire will be flat in a minute or two."

Sissy had brought her Canon Powershot digital camera, hoping to get a photo of the license plate. But to their surprise it had been removed. Just a metal bracket with empty screw holes. That seemed like proof positive the driver was up to no good.

Well, if she couldn't get a picture of the car's license plate, she would get one of the driver. He was likely Madame Flora's confident. N'yen had been pretty sure this guy in the car was the one transmitting his voice into the cupola where the séance was taking place.

Inching her way to the front of the car, Sissy climbed onto the chrome bumper, pointed the camera toward the driver, and shouted, "Say cheese!"

F-l-s-s-k!

The flash startled the man behind the wheel. He raised his hand to shade his eyes, dropping the microphone. "What the blazes –?" he yelled.

Sissy took off running, heading down the hill, clutching the small red camera firmly in her hand. "Yippee Ki Yay," she shouted, an abbreviated version of Bruce Willis's famous line in *Die Hard*. She may have been too polite to say it out loud, but she finished the quote in her head.

Behind her, she heard the Buick roar to life. The tires hummed on the road behind her. Gaining speed, like a bull coming after a matador. Holy moly, it was going to run her down.

By the time Sissy realized her escape route left her vulnerable, it was too late to change course. The grassy shoulders were steep, practically a cliff on each side of the paved road. There was nowhere to go but down the hill. And she couldn't outrun the speeding car behind her.

As often happened when Sissy became frightened, she dropped to the pavement and curled into a fetal position – "like a roly-poly bug," Aggie often teased her. It was a nervous reaction she'd had since early childhood, an ostrich-like reaction akin to burying her head in the sand. "Jesus, save me," she prayed aloud, eyes tightly closed, arms wrapped around her knees.

The Buick was upon her. The headlights focused on her curled-up form like the beam of a ray gun. She knew she was going to die!

Then suddenly the car served, one tire hitting the shoulder of the road. The big behemoth of an automobile screeched to a stop, just short of going over the side of the hill. The flat rear tire had halted it in its tracks.

The Buick's front wheels had barely missed her. She could feel the heat of the engine from where she lay. Hear its ticking. Sense its metallic closeness.

Sissy leapt to her feet and took off running again, making it to the bottom of High Jinks Hill and hiding behind an oak tree before the Buick came lumbering slowly down the incline, riding on a rim. She watched the sparks fly from the metal grinding against the pavement as the car moved down Fourth Street and turned a corner, disappearing from sight.

"Are you all right?" Aggie shouted as she came racing down the hill, arms waving. "I thought that flat tire would hold him."

Sissy stepped from behind the thick tree, breathing a sigh of relief. "At least it stopped him short of running over me."

"Just barely. I sure thought you were a goner!"

"Well, it's his goose that's barbequed," Sissy said. "I got a picture of him. Straight-on through the windshield."

"C'mon, N'yen can help us download it onto a thumb drive and we can take it to the police first thing in the morning. Madame Flora going to be none too happy when we expose her partner in crime."

~ ~ ~

N'yen downloaded the contents of Sissy's digital camera onto one of his computers – he had seven – and opened the jpg images. There were about half a dozen pictures, most of them of her cat Mittens. It was the last photo that interested him.

"Can you see his face?" asked Sissy.

"You blew it," sighed the boy. "The flash reflected off the windshield making it a big blotch of white."

"What?"

Aggie peered over his shoulder. "That's a nice photo of Mittens," she said. "But just a glare instead of the man in the car."

"You mean I almost got run over for nothing?"

"I'm afraid so," said N'yen. "Good try, but you guys blew it."

"Drat!" said Sissy. But she was thinking of harsher words.

N'yen yawned. "Now you girls go back to your own wing. It's two o'clock in the morning and I'm going to bed."

"Well, okay," said Aggie. "But we confirmed one thing."

"What's that?"

"That Madame Flora's up to something shady. Why else would her henchman try to run over Sissy?"

Chapter Twenty-Eight

Setting the Snare

"**W**e've got her," said Beau Madison. "She demanded a million dollars. Uh, well, her so-called spirit did."

"Hold on a gosh-darned minute," said Chief Jim Purdue. "This is not as simple as it seems."

The two men were sitting there in the police chief's office, hunched over a digital recorder about the size of a cigarette pack that Jim Purdue had used to wire his friend for last night's séance.

"What's the problem?"

"This is not exactly a blackmail demand. The ghost is trying to sell you a quilt. Maybe a million dollars is a high price, but he's simply offering to sell you something for a stated price. No law against that."

"Yeah, but —"

"The conversation on this digital recorder has nothing to do with your great-grandfather killing some dude or threating to expose any family secrets if you don't pay up."

"But it's a clever ruse, don't you see?" exclaimed Beau. Despite his taciturn demeanor, he could become quite agitated if provoked. "The offer to sell me that quilt is just code for paying him to keep quiet."

"Maybe so. But it might be hard to convince a jury of that. Best we can do is run them in for fortune telling. You've got clear proof of that on this recording."

"But that quilt's not even real. What else could it be?"

"They might be trying to sell you a phony quilt that they're passing off as the real thing. Remember, Florence Bashinski and her husband Heinrich are grifters. They have a rap sheet longer than college professor's resume. Petty crimes, con jobs, fortune telling scams, posing as IRS agents, snatch-and-grab, that sort of thing. They were once arrested for trying to sell the Brooklyn Bridge – literally."

"Maybe I should show up at the diner at noon and see what the guy's trying to pass off as the Tristan Quilt," said Beau.

"Not a bad idea. I'll wire you up again. Better take Lizzie with you. She'd know the real thing from a copy."

"Think she'd go?"

"Lizzie? The way that gal likes to get in on the town's hot gossip, she'd probably pay you to take her along. I'll give her a call and set it up for noon."

"Think we oughta tell Edgar we're using his wife for undercover police work?"

"We won't be able to reach him this morning. He was going birdwatching up near Injun Woods. There's not much of a phone signal in that area."

"Birdwatching? Maybe with a 12-guage pump-action shotgun."

"Yeah, well, quail season doesn't start till November 1st. His birdwatching may be a bit premature here in the middle of the summer. I told him to at least carry a pair of binoculars in case he meets a game warden. I'm tired of interceding for him."

"You better call Lizzie now. It will take her a good two hours to get ready, if I know that fussy lady."

"She can be a bit vain, truth be told."

"Lizzie was that way in high school too. The first girl to wear lipstick."

"But it did look good with that red hair. I would've asked her out if Edgar hadn't beat me to it."

"We all wound up with the right wives," affirmed Beau with a quiet chuckle. His narrow face crossed with a grin.

"That's a true fact.," nodded Jim as he glanced at the clock on the wall. "It's ten-fifteen. Lizzie should be at the Quilting Heritage Museum by now. It's supposed to open at ten, Monday through Friday."

"When she doesn't sleep late."

~ ~ ~

Lizzie Ridenour was more than willing to play Mata Hari. But she had to look good for the part, so she hung a CLOSED sign on the museum's door and hurried home to change clothes and adjust her makeup.

She and Edgar lived on River Road in a big colonnaded house overlooking the Wabash. Designed to look like Tara from *Gone With the Wind*, it suited her pretentious nature. She loved that movie, even if it wasn't PC to admit that anymore.

Before undertaking the ritual of "getting ready," she phoned each of her friends in turn – Maddy, Bootsie, Cookie – to discuss how she should act at the meeting with Madame Flora's accomplice. Aloof? Stern? Friendly? Frosty?

They settled on 'Authoritative.' After all, she was there as a quilt expert, checking to see if his Tristan Quilt was the real thing. She should look confident and knowledgeable.

She and Cookie were betting it was the real deal. Maddy and Bootsie were skeptical.

~ ~ ~

At that moment, Sissy Jackson sat across from Chief Jim Purdue. Aggie had insisted her friend tell the police about the car that tried to run her down last night.

"So that's how they do it," said Jim Purdue. "Radio transmission from a nearby car."

"It was a Buick of some kind," said Aggie, sitting in the chair next to her friend. They were in the police chief's cramped office. He'd sent a deputy next door to Cozy Café to buy Pepsis for both girls. Maybe some donuts, too.

151

"What kind of Buick?" Chief Purdue asked Aggie.

"Dunno. But it was blue. Kinda rusty."

"Anything else?"

"It didn't have a license plate."

Chief Purdue turned his attention back to Sissy. "You say you took a photo of the driver?"

"Yessir, but it didn't turn out. The flash reflected on the windshield. All I got was a big white blob."

"But you saw him."

"Un-huh."

"Think you'd recognize him if you saw him again?"

"Un-huh."

Can you describe him?"

"Un-huh."

"Well –?"

"He was baldheaded and had a painted-on moustache."

"Painted on?"

"I mean it *looked* painted on. Thin, like you'd get if you drew a moustache with an eyeliner pencil."

"Anything else?"

"No, I couldn't see much of him. He was practically hidden behind the steering wheel. Like he was short, a little fellow, barely able to see over the dashboard."

"Hmm, that should make him easy to identify. But I've not seen anybody around town who fits that description."

Aggie spoke up. "He's obviously working with Madame Flora. Does she have a boyfriend?"

"An ex-husband."

"Can you get a picture of him?" asked Sissy. "I could identify him from a picture, I think."

"Sure. He's got a record. I'll ask Indy to email his mugshot to us." Jim Purdue reached for the telephone.

"If you catch him, can you arrest him for trying to run me over?" asked Sissy. "It scared me something terrible. I wet my pants."

"TMI," whispered Aggie to her friend.

Chapter Twenty-Nine

The Meeting

Maisie Walters gave Beau and Lizzie the corner booth. The proprietress of Cozy Café was being extra careful during the pandemic, despite the town having been vaccinated with two doses of the Modern Times formulation. Masks were required when not eating. Tables were spread six-feet apart. Hours were restricted.

You couldn't be too careful. No telling when someone from out of town might stop by for a meal. Mayor Mark Tidemore – her nephew by marriage – had told her it might not be legal to post a sign in front of the diner saying LOCALS ONLY. So she took the temperature of each diner as they came in through the revolving glass door.

Beau and Lizzie ordered coffee and a slice of watermelon pie. It wouldn't be proper to take up seats at the diner without ordering anything, although Maisie would have allowed them any latitude they wanted. As Maddy's twin sister, she was more than willing to extend privileges to her brother-in-law.

Beau kept glancing at the neon clock on the far wall: 12:10. He wondered of this Luigi Guicciardini was going to be a no-show.

Just when his patience was reaching its end – 12:15 – the revolving door admitted a short baldheaded man with a thin moustache. He wore a suit that looked like it had just come off the rack at Goodwill. He looked around, spotted them and made a beeline to their booth.

"You Beauregard Madison?"

"I am," Beau said, surreptitiously flicking on the switch to the recorder in his jacket pocket.

"Who's the fancy broad?"

"I beg your pardon?" said Lizzie. Eyebrows knitting in anger. She'd worked very diligently on her makeup.

Beau interceded. "This is the director of the local quilting museum. We're buying the Tristan Quilt to donate to the museum. The Hoople Trust Fund is putting up the money because it wants to create an attraction that will bring more visitors to the town." He patted the sleek leather attaché case on the vinyl seat next to him as if it contained the million dollars.

"We – uh, I mean me – I was selling the quilt sight unseen. Nobody said anything about it being inspected by a museum expert."

"Simply want to make sure we're getting what we're paying for. Where is the quilt?"

"In my car trunk, like the spirit told you."

"How did you come by this piece of the Tristan Quilt?"

"Been in my family for years. I'm a relative of the Count that your great-grandfather shot back in 1832."

"You're Italian?" The man looked more Slavic to Beau.

"Yeah, sure. My name's Luigi, ain't it?"

"I don't know. Do you have any identification?"

"Uh, I left it at home."

"Can we see the quilt?"

"Tell you what – you give me half the money to show your good faith, and I'll give you the quilt so your lady here can go off and inspect it. When she confirms its authenticity, you pay me the other half. That a fair deal?"

"And if the quilt doesn't pass muster, we get the five hundred thousand back?"

"Sure. I'm an honest guy, right? I'll meet you right here at noon tomorrow. You bring the other five hundred thousand if the quilt's on the up and up. If not, I hand you your good faith money back."

Beau smiled pleasantly, as if happy with this risky arrangement. He could see why they called guys like this "confidence" men. "Okay, go get the quilt while I count out the money."

"You got a million bucks in that attaché case?"

"Yes, I went by the bank first thing this morning."

"Sit right there and I'll be back in a jiffy."

Beau and Lizzie waited twenty minutes till realizing the man wasn't coming back. Beau clicked off the recorder.

"He smelled a rat," Lizzie said.

She was right about that.

Heinrich Bashinski might be a little crude, but he knew a thing or two about money. His profession depended on this knowledge. Switching a *bujo* for a bag of worthless paper took a certain know-how. You had to get the size and dimensions exactly right.

A million dollars in one hundred dollar bills would take up a standard 17-inch briefcase. A little tight but it would fit. But that amount of money would *never* fit into a slender attaché case.

Heinrich drove back to Helga's Hideaway, looking over his shoulder all the while for a cop car. He'd walked into a setup back there at the diner.

Jeez, that was close, he told himself

Chapter Thirty

A Lost Sketchbook

Helga Hoople couldn't find one of her favorite sketchbooks, a collection of charcoal drawings of cottontail rabbits and fox squirrels and stray coyotes and beaver and badgers. One even of a wolf.

Early settlers had eliminated wolves from the state by 1908. In recent history, only a single gray wolf has been sighted, although it is believed young males from a Wisconsin pack sometimes pass through. These stray wolves don't stay long because they are unable to find a mate.

Midwestern gray wolves are smaller than Western and Alaska gray wolves, but are still more than twice the weight of an average coyote. Rumors about the mating of wolves and coyotes – producing a coywolf – are false, according to Indiana state wildlife authorities. But wolves (*Canis lupus*), coyotes (*Canis latrans*), and domestic dogs (*Canis familiaris*) are closely-related species. All three can interbreed and produce viable, fertile offspring — wolfdogs, coywolves, and coydogs. These combinations are becoming more and more common throughout the Midwest. In fact, the red wolf has been shown by DNA testing to be a coyote-wolf hybrid.

Wolves in Indiana are protected under federal law. State law allows a resident to kill a wolf if it poses a threat to people or while it is causing damage to property. Not that there are any wolves to protect – making the law seem somewhat superfluous.

Historic records are scarce, but wolf packs were prevalent in the early 1800s. Indiana was home to both gray and red wolf populations. Pioneers hunted wolves to protect their livestock from these howling packs of predators.

However, wolves attacking humans is so rare as to be nearly mythical, mostly emanating from European and Russian folktales of the 1600s.

But it did happen.

So Helga had kept her distance while sketching this oversized canine. It stood there watching her, almost as if posing. The drawing had turned out well, one of her better pieces.

Now she couldn't find the drawing. It had to be around somewhere. Then, it occurred to her that she may have left the sketchbook behind at the cabin she had lived in before rejoining her sister at the Hoople Mansion.

Everybody had assumed she was dead, but thanks to the help of a few close friends she remained hidden, surviving on occasional food deliveries, occupying herself with sketching and painting, and quiltmaking.

"Hilda," she called to her sister, "would you like to drive up to my old hideaway with me today? I think I left something there."

~ ~ ~

Later that morning Deputy Harry Teague pulled his police cruiser onto the rutted sideroad that led up to Helga's Hideaway. He figured this was going to be a wild goose chase, so he didn't worry about being sighted by anyone at the shack where Helga Hoople had lived while playing the hermit. Buck Jackson probably had mistook a couple of high school kids looking for a place to make out for the fortune teller and her partner. He was sure this was a waste of time, but when Chief Purdue said go, he went!

That's why Harry was surprised to see two cars parked in front of the squat building – an old grey-colored Rolls Royce and a rusty blue Buick. Killing his engine, he stepped out of the cruiser, hand near his revolver. "Hello," he called. "Who's there. This is private property."

The two elderly women stepped outside under the little portico that served as a porch, although it did little to protect them from the summer sun. "Oh, it's all right," replied Helga Hoople. "I own this place."

"Actually, I do,' corrected her sister Hilda. "You were declared dead, remember? I inherited everything."

"Well, I'm feeling quite alive today," insisted the other. "I came out here to retrieve my sketchbook." She held up a large spiral-bound pad identified by the brand name of Grumbacher. "And here it is. It was in the cabinet where I left it."

"You ladies driving two cars?"

"My lord, no," gushed Aunt Hilda. "I'm not even supposed to be driving one car. They took away my license last year. But Helga insisted I bring her up here. We don't keep a driver on staff anymore."

Harry Teague inspected the other car, a 2016 Buick Lacrosse. An extra tire lay near it, the rubber chewed up from driving on the rim. A jack was next to it. The Buick was obviously driving on the spare. Also, the car had no license plate.

Something funny going on here. "Whose car is this one?" he asked.

Hilda Hoople glanced toward the Buick. "Oh, that automobile belongs to Mr. Smith. He's inside the cabin. He will be staying here a few days."

"Did you give him permission?"

"No, but I don't mind," said Helga. "I don't use the place anymore."

"Was he here when you arrived?"

"Yes, it was quite a surprise. But he explained that he rented it through Air B&B. I didn't even know we had it listed with that service. Probably something Barney did to make us extra money. Penny wise and all that."

Teague recognized the name. Barnabas Soltairé was manager of the Hoople Trust. But all cops knew him by reputation. He used to be the lawyer for the Indy mob. "Maybe I better say hello to your guest. Make sure he's comfortable."

"Dear me, we want him to have a nice stay," said Aunt Hilda.

"Yes indeed," echoed Aunt Helga.

Deputy Harry Teague drew his service pistol as he stepped into the cabin. Air B&B, my ass, he thought.

~ ~ ~

"That's him," Beau identified the prisoner that Deputy Teague brought in just before noon. "Said his name was Luigi Guicciardini."

Lizzie nodded. "Yes, that's the man who tried to sell us the quilt. But he took off when we asked a few questions."

"This man matches the mug shots we have of Henry Bashinski, a small-time confidence man from Indianapolis. The Indy police emailed us the mugshot. They have a BOLO on him as a person of interest in the murder of an autograph dealer named Robert Roberts. He's the husband of –"

"Ex-husband," Heinrich spoke up for the first time.

"Whatever – of Florence Bashinski, also known as Madame Flora," Chief Purdue completed his sentence.

"Look, I didn't kill anybody," the prisoner said. "Florence shot Robert Bob Roberts to get that letter that told us about the Tristan Quilt."

"So it is real?" Lizzie leaned forward, all ears.

"Beats me," said Heinrich. "All I know is what the letter from that Count said."

~ ~ ~

Police Chief Jim Purdue sent another deputy over to the Mansion to arrest Heinrich Bashinski's wife or ex-wife or whatever she was. Partner in crime might be the better term.

Florence Bashinski didn't go peacefully, so Deputy Tommy Truehart put the cuffs on her. Searching her room (with Aunt Hilda's permission) he turned up the laser pointer and the tiny transmitter. Evidence of a fraud.

Back at the police station, ol' Heinrich was talking, blaming everything on "Madame Flora," claiming she masterminded the whole thing, that he was merely an innocent pawn caught up in his ex-wife's machinations.

"How did you know about the silver bullet?" asked Beau Madison, hoping for a better answer than he got from the ghost.

"It was mentioned in a book. Some scribblings in the margin."

"Where is this book?" demanded Beau.

"In my lock box at the local bank. Put it there for safekeeping. Don't want to leave a five-grand document laying around, now do I?"

"Is the letter there too?" asked Chief Purdue.

"Yeah, it's there. The letter and the book."

"What kind of book is this?" Beau wanted to know.

"A journal by that guy this town's named after. The margins are covered with handwriting. They were written there by that mayor fellow who was a relative of some sort. Guess it was his thoughts about the old man's stories, some notations that added to the town's history."

"That must be *My Journey into Indian Territory, 1829* by Jacob Caruthers. Henry Caruthers did a private printing," said Beau. "We've got a copy at home, but it doesn't have any handwriting in the margins."

Heinrich looked up defiantly. "Well, there's plenty of writing in the book I have in my lock box."

"If you've got a key to that bank lock box, hand it over," ordered Chief Purdue, holding out his hand, palm up.

Heinrich fished in his pocket and retrieved a brass key. "Here you go. Enjoy reading about your esteemed Town Founders. Col. Madison was a cold-blooded murderer, by all accounts. Shot that poor Count dead after the duel was already over. You should've paid me to keep it quiet."

"Little late for that now. The ghost of my forebear – you, I assume – blabbed it out to a roomful of the biggest gossips in the town."

"I thought I gave a good performance."

"Not really. My great-grandfather would never have called me 'laddie.' And you had Arthur Conan Doyle all wrong. I'm a big fan of his Sherlock Holmes books, so I know something about him. Doyle didn't speak with a Cockney accent."

"Says you. I played Dr. Watson in a stage production of *Sherlock Holmes: The Musical*. Florence played Professor Moriarty's daughter Bella. We got a standing ovation."

Beau turned to the Police Chief. "I want to see that book with all the handwriting," he said.

Jim Purdue slapped the key down on his desk. There was barely space for it among all the corner-to-corner clutter – daily call reports, pink message slips, official BOLO alerts, FBI wanted posters, state police bulletins, and the like. "We'll check it out tomorrow," he promised. "First thing tonight, I've got to go clear out a cell. Jasper Beanie's sleeping one off in the back cell. He treats the place like a home-away-from-home B&B. Time for him to go home to his own bed."

"Just one thing," pleaded Heinrich Bashinski.

"What's that?"

"Don't put me in a cell with my wife. She'll kill me like she did that manuscript dealer."

~ ~ ~

Bootsie heard about the arrests when she brought her husband dinner. He had called to say he was working late. She had made Watermelon & Lamb Stew, one of his favorites.

Afterward, Bootsie called Maddy who called Cookie who called Lizzy. Then Maddy told Leslie Ann and Aggie. And Aggie told N'yen.

They all agreed to meet immediately on the front steps of Caruthers Corners Savings & Loan.

Chapter Thirty-One

The Big Break-In

That night, the Quilters Club robbed a bank.

It wasn't very difficult, as it turned out. Lizzie Ridenour had a key to the front door of Caruthers Corners Savings & Loan. Not because she was the bank's largest shareholder, but because her husband – the bank's former president – forgot to turn in his set of keys when he retired. Nobody had bothered to change the locks since 1954, when a drunken watermelon farmer named Wyeth Willet threw a rock through the glass door. He'd been angry that the bank had bounced his check. The new lock had served its purpose for 67 years just fine, no need for changing.

The gang of burglars – including Lady Greystone and the kids – followed Lizzie across the marble-floored lobby, past the empty tellers' cages, and into the large safe deposit room next to the vault. She had a key for it too –the room, not the vault. The vault worked on a timer.

Lizzie had paused at the bank manager's desk to type a password into a computer that allowed her to access the database of safe deposit box renters. The password was the same as it had been when Edgar worked there: CaruthersCorners 1234.

Not very secure, but the town had little crime.

She quickly identified the box rented to Heinrich Bashinski –1712 – and found the bank's matching key on the series of hooks where they were kept.

"Now here's where it gets trickier," Lizzie said to the assembled bank robbers. "I don't have a second key to any of these boxes." It took two keys to open the box, she explained. And Heinrich's key was in police custody.

"Not to worry," said Bootsie, holding up a brass key that was an exact duplicate of the one in Lizzie's hand. "I picked this up off Jim's desk when I brought him supper at the police station tonight. He's working late, what with two prisoners in his little jail. They had to kick Jasper Beanie out of one of the holding cells to make room for Madame Flora."

"Florence Bashinski, you mean," corrected Maddy. "That's her real name according to her driver's license." She'd glimpsed the license when Deputy Tommy Truehart arrested the woman at the Manson earlier tonight. He'd found it in her purse.

"Hurry up, everybody," urged Lizzie. "It wouldn't do for me to get arrested for breaking into my own bank."

"I'm not worried for myself," chirped Lady Greystone. "I have diplomatic immunity."

"And I'm an underaged child," said Aggie smugly.

"No, you're not," countered Bootsie. "In Indiana, anyone age 10 or older can be tried in adult court." You don't stay married to a policeman for forty-plus years without some knowledge of the law rubbing off on you.

"That's right," nodded Cookie, calling on her eidetic memory. "We're all at risk. Except maybe for Leslie Ann."

"Yes, but me getting arrested for bank robbery would cause quite a scandal. Oliver would be most unhappy with my behavior."

"I'll get kicked out of the graduate program at Northwestern if I get arrested for robbing a bank," moaned N'yen.

"And my grandfather would ground me forever," whined Sissy Jackson.

"Better hurry up then," Aggie changed her tune. "We don't want to get caught. It would be bad for everyone."

"Quiet, please," Lizzie shushed them, as if she were a librarian calling for silence in the Reading Room. "And turn off your flashlights. We don't want to attract the attention of any passersby."

Bootsie inserted her key in one of the locks on box 1712 and turned it with a satisfying *click*! Lizzie did the same with the bank's key, another *click*! Then they slid the long metal box out of its slot and raised the lid.

"What's that?" asked Cookie.

"Looks like a letter," said Maddy. "And a book."

Chapter Thirty-Two

The Undelivered Letter

Maddy unfolded the yellowed letter and read:

Dear Mario,

> Signore, mio Dio, io ti ringrazio
> che hai portato a termine questo giorno;
> io ti ringrazio che hai dato riposo al corpo e all'anima.

I am writing to you in regard to the linen fabric swatch that your brother Allessandro (my favorite cousin) asked me to deliver to you on my journey to San Francisco. However, Fate has intervened and I may not be able to comply with my promise.

Three events have interfered –

The first is the breakdown of the wagon train on which I had purchased passage. This has stranded me here in the new American state of Indiana. I have already written to you about this.

The second event is that three days ago I was attacked by a vicious wolf while hunting. The injury refuses to heal and I suffer a great fever, which leaves me confused and my mind in a state of turmoil. My head pounds heavily and I have difficulty drinking water. Nausea overcomes me. Medical help is wanting in this remote encampment. The infection is uncontrolled. I fear I may die from this injury.

The third is a quarrel with one of the wagon masters who stranded me here. I have demanded onward passage to San Francisco, for which I have done paid, but he refuses to honor the debt. I have been left with no choice but to challenge him to a duel, the settlement to be made out of his estate if I win, the debt forgiven if I die. The downside of this course of action is that I am a poor shot and he is an experienced Indian fighter, said to be most proficient with firearms.

My lack of expertise if confounded by the woozy state of mind I endure from my hunting injury. I carry my gun at all times.

Knowing that I may not be able to fulfill my mission of delivering Allessandro's package to you, I have decided to place it with a friend for safekeeping. I mentioned him in my previous letter, the fat redheaded farmer who has claimed acreage to the north. If you indeed travel here, he will have this family heirloom in his keeping. It is yours for the asking. The fabric swatch is very valuable, a piece of the Tristan and Isolde Quilt.

A Gesù

Antonio

The letter's envelope told the story. It was stamped:

RETURNED FOR
POSTAGE DUE

Count Guicciardini had sent the letter to his cousin in San Francisco, but it never arrived. Stopped by the post mistress in nearby Vincennes. Returned for improper postage, the letter had come back after the Count was dead. So Mario

Guicciardini never knew that the quilt fragment was being held for him by the Count's friend – "the fat redheaded farmer."

Chapter Thirty-Three

The Annotated Journal

Beau ran his finger down the pages of Jacob Caruthers' journal, the annotated copy that the gals had found in the safe deposit box. It was a typeset version of the handwritten original on display at the Historical Society. Difference here was a fine, feathery script in the margins, an addition by ol' Jacob's great-grandson, Henry Caruthers. This must have been Henry's personal copy with his own notations.

On page 73 he read:

> The Colonel got forced into a duel by that pesky Count who refused to accept the work of Providence that left him stranded here in our new settlement. Beauregard won the contest, of course.

In the margin, Henry Caruthers had written in black ink:

> *Jacob Caruthers served as the Colonel's second. He said Beauregard Madison killed the Count with a silver bullet to the heart. An odd choice of weaponry. Shot him after the duel had ended, but no one complained about the unpopular Italian's demise. Col. Madison clearly got away with murder.*

There it was. The silver bullet. That's where Madame Flora and her husband got that bit of theatrical embellishment.

Beau thumbed through all 224 pages of the journal, but there was no mention of the Tristan Quilt. That bit of information obviously came from Count Antonio Guicciardini's undelivered letter.

Henry Caruthers' other annotations merely amplified his own skewed observations of history, interpreting every event in his ancestor's favor – painting Col. Madison as an undeserving ruffian and dismissing Ferdinand Jinks as an inconsequential bystander. Major Samuel Beasley was reduced to being an "Indian killer" and Rev. Thaddeus Taylor a deranged "Bible Thumper." He described Andrew Wayne and Sgt. Abraham Duncan as a pair of "horse thieves" and Wild Man John Longbottom as a "slaughterer of buffalo, beaver, and birds." The only person mentioned with kindness was Sir Samuel Langston Buttersworth, "a fine gentleman unfairly killed by that mongrel Mordicai Bradshaw over a lame horse."

Henry Caruthers concluded his annotations with the following words:

> *One day history will credit my ancestor with single-handedly raising this town from the mud and dust of the Wabash River basin. And I will be seen as his rightful successor.*

Didn't work out that way. Former mayor Henry Caruthers was serving a prison sentence at Pendleton for embezzlement. Dipping into the town's coffers. He was just as much a scallywag as his long-ago ancestor.

~ ~ ~

Police Chief Jim Purdue had to lie down. He wondered if he was having a heart attack or a stroke or a mental breakdown. Both dispatchers – Elvina and her sister Myrtle – hovered over him like ER nurses. Tommy Truehart ran next door to get ice for his forehead from Cozy Café. Harry Teague suggested they call Doc Medford, but he wouldn't hear of it.

"I can't get my breath," he wheezed. His face looked like a red balloon about to pop. His eyed bulged like a pair of Ping Pong balls. He didn't look healthy.

"There, there," soothed Elvina. "You'll be okay in a minute."

"That's right," said Myrtle. "Just try to relax,"

Everybody knew Jim Purdue was merely having an anxiety attack. He had flown into a temper fit when he heard

174

that the Quilters Club had gone into the bank on their own. Not only did those intruders include his own wife, but also the bank's largest shareholder, the mayor's mother-in-law, the wife of the county's largest landholder, three children, and a foreign national.

"What am I gonna do?" he moaned. "Throw my own wife into jail? Cause an international incident with a member of British royalty? Arrest all my friend's wives?"

Deputy Teague leaned closer. "Here's my advice, Chief. Do nothing."

"Huh? But I have a duty to –"

"Let it go. This was just a group of well-meaning citizens who retrieved evidence in a murder case and turned it over to the proper authority – meaning you. The Indy police will appreciate your help in solving a murder case. You'll get the credit, your name in the paper."

"But –"

"Maybe your friends bent the law a tad, but no harm, no foul. Let it go."

"Yes, but –"

"Take a deep breath, walk around the block, then give a statement to the *Burpyville Gazette* thanking everybody for their support of the local police. Describe them as a neighborhood watch group. Praise their civic contribution to law and order. Turn this lemon into lemonade."

The Chief sat up, shaking his head. "You're right," he said, his breathing returning closer to normal. "We got the bad guys, with a little help from the public. All's well that ends well."

Chapter Thirty-Four
Passing Along the Family Secret

Beau decided to skip a generation – and the bloodline – in passing along the family secret. His oldest son Bill wouldn't have a clue what to make of a wild story about werewolves and silver bullets. But Bill's adopted son N'yen would. The little genius had a curious mind, absorbing knowledge like a Bounty paper towel soaking up a spill. And besides, he was the only male grandson.

Sure, this business of passing knowledge and inheritance and privilege along to male heirs was sexist. Always had been. But that was the tradition. And Beauregard Madison was, if nothing else, a traditionalist. A descendent of a Founding Father of Caruthers Corners.

That accident of birth created a certain responsibility to maintain the thread of history. And this little Indiana town thrived on its historical annals more than most. The three rough-and-tumble pioneers who led the wagon train here were honored with statues and celebrations. The town was named after one of them. Descendants of those early pioneers formed the backbone of the town's society. The yearly Watermelon Days festival featured a parade honoring the Town's Founders. To Beau, it was a duty.

Maddy was more iconoclastic. Her own lineage had shifted from a direct connection with the Founders to a hodgepodge of charlatans, crazies, and artificial family ties. She respected her husband's devotion to the past; she had her own eye to times gone by. But to her history was a series of mysteries to be unraveled; to Beau it was an immutable link to the present.

~ ~ ~

Beau Madison took his grandson fishing, a longtime ritual. However, this trip Beau's pal Edgar Ridenour found an excuse to allow the boy and old man some private time together, professing to have to attend a board meeting for the savings and loan that he used to manage. Apparently, there had been a break-in. Security had to be tightened.

The 20-foot Roughneck 2070 SC was easy to handle. By now, the 16-year-old Vietnamese boy could navigate the boat on the shallow waters of the Wabash as proficiently as the adults. They let the boat drift near the 101 bridge, a deeper spot inhabited by Ol' Calvin, an elusive catfish. But today no hooks were dipped into the water. Beau was there to impart a piece of history – family tradition – to his grandson.

"You know the story of how the town was founded when a wagon train broke down here in 1829?"

"Of course, Grampy. Everybody around here knows that story."

"And you also know that my great-grandfather – that would be your great-great-great-grandfather – was one of the three leaders of that wagon train."

"My great-great-great-grandfather, even though I'm adopted?" N'yen still remembered his original parents.

"You're a part of this family now."

"Yes, Grampy."

"That's why I'm going to tell you a story that Madison men pass along to their sons – or in this case – grandson."

"Does it have to do with that silver bullet?"

"It does."

"Does it have to be a secret?"

"It does. Because people will think you're crazy if you repeat the story outside the family."

"Okay."

"Like you guessed, it has to do with that silver bullet. You see, Col. Madison – the first Beauregard Hollingsworth Madison – used that bullet to kill a werewolf."

"You're saying the Count was a werewolf?"

"That's what Col. Madison believed. According to the story he passed along to his son and his son passed to my father and my father to me –"

"– and now you to me."

"Yes. According to Col. Madison, following their duel, the Count transformed into a slavering wolf-man and attacked him."

"What was the duel about?"

"The Count was angry that he'd paid for passage to San Francisco, but only got as far as Indiana. He wanted his money back," explained Beau.

"What happened in the duel?"

"According to the story, the Count fired first. But his hand was badly trembling and he missed. The Colonel raised his pistol and fired into the air, ending the matter. Nobody died in the duel."

"Then what happened." N'yen's eyes were wide as he leaned forward from his seat in the aluminum boat, not wanting to miss a word. The sunlight pushed through the overhead trees, sparkling on the water. The birds were quiet in the surrounding forest.

Beau cleared his throat. "According to the story, the Colonel began to reload his flintlock pistol in case his opponent chose to continue the dispute. The man was acting strangely."

"Yes?"

"Suddenly, the Count let out a great growl and rushed toward the Colonel. The Count's second, a man named Archibald Aitken, tried to hold him back, but the Count shook him off like a dog shaking water. Colonel Madison told his son that the Count's face was distorted into that of a wild beast, his teeth were bared, his eyes blood-red, and he was foaming at the mouth. Recognizing that he was dealing with a supernatural beast, he completed loading his flintlock, but snatching off his silver wedding ring he stuffed it into the barrel and added wadding."

"Wow! What happened next, Grampy?"

"Archibald Aitken delayed the Count's rush long enough for the Colonel to finish loading his pistol, raise it, and fire directly into the werewolf's heart. Stopped him in his tracks a mere three feet from where the Colonel stood his ground. Killed him dead."

"That's redundant, Grampy. If he killed him he would by definition be dead."

"You know what I mean. Your great-great-great-grandfather killed a werewolf."

"So you're saying this Count from Europe was a real-life, honest-to-goodness wolfman – really?"

"I'm not saying that. But Col. Madison did."

"There's a medical term for this condition. It's called Lycanthropy. This usually refers to victims of congenital porphyria, a rare hereditary disease in which the blood pigment hemoglobin is abnormally metabolized. Symptoms include sensitivity to light, reddish teeth, dark pee, and psychosis. That might be seen as being a werewolf."

"How do you know this stuff?" asked his grandfather.

"I read."

"Porphyria – I suppose that could explain it."

"There's another condition called Hypertrichosis. It's sometimes called the 'Wolfman Syndrome.' This is an excessive hair growth over the body. Congenital, the condition is usually accompanied by gingival hyperplasia, an increase in the size of the gums, causing the teeth to protrude."

"That would be pretty weird."

"In the 19ᵗʰ and 20ᵗʰ Centuries, people who suffered from this hirsute condition often wound up as circus sideshow performers. Jesús 'Chuy' Aceves was known as the Wolf Boy. Julia Pastrana was promoted as the Monkey Girl."

"Do you think the Count suffered from one of these conditions?"

"Nope. I think the explanation was much simpler."

"Like what?"

"The Count's undelivered letter said he'd been bit by a wolf."

"And that turned him into a werewolf?"

"No, Grampy. I think the wolf was rabid. The Count's symptoms sound like his was in the final stages of rabies. So don't feel bad that the Colonel shot him. At that stage – foaming at the mouth, psychotic aggression – he would have died anyway. Rabies is a viral disease, an inflammation of the brain. Once symptoms appear, the result is nearly always fatal."

"Rabies? You mean Hydrophobia?"

"It's sometimes called that because one of the symptoms is a supposed fear of water. In the later stages of an infection the victim has difficulty swallowing and being unable to quench his thirst he panics when presented with liquids to drink."

"Jeez, you must read a lot."

"Grammy always said, 'Reading brings knowledge and knowledge is power; therefore reading is power. The power to know and learn and understand ... but also the power to dream.' She got that from some book she read, but she said those were good words to live by."

"Hmm, I've heard her say the same thing."

Chapter Thirty-Five

Climbing Family Trees

C ookie didn't have to consult the genealogy charts that she kept at the Historical Society. With her trick memory, she could call up every limb on every family tree in Caruthers Corners. "Yep," she said. "Archibald Reginald Aitkens was a forbearer of Floyd Aitken, founder of Aitkens Produce. Floyd is survived by a son and daughter. The son moved away last year, but his daughter Susanne is married to Peter Paul Hitzer."

"Then, I suggest we pay a visit to Old McDonald's Dairy," said Maddy as she served slices of her Watermelon Upside Down Cake to the Quilters Club there in the parlor of the Hoople Mansion.

"Petie and Susy Q took over the dairy when his parents retired to Florida," Bootsie explained to Leslie Ann. Bootsie and Jim's little bungalow backed up to the dairy farm's west pasture, making them neighbors.

"Yes, let's pay them a visit," nodded Lizzie.

"I thought we were under House Arrest for robbing the bank," said Aggie, helping herself to an extra slice of cake.

"Not legally," replied her cousin N'yen. "We didn't get arrested. It was just a warning to stay out of trouble. Uncle Jim said we should stay put."

"They couldn't arrest me for robbing my own bank," sniffed Lizzie. "I *am* the largest shareholder. And we didn't steal anything."

"Just that ol' letter and Jacob Caruthers' journal," said Sissy.

"We didn't actually steal them," corrected Bootsie. "We merely confiscated those items and turned them over to the police. They are in my husband's custody as we speak."

"Yes, after we read them," Cookie added for accuracy. She was fussy about details like that.

"So our getting those documents was sort of like making a citizen's arrest?" asked Aggie.

"Well, kinda like that," laughed her grandmother. "As good citizens, we took action to secure that letter and book."

"Nonetheless, Jim threatened to arrest us for interfering with a police investigation," Cookie pointed out. "He was awfully mad."

"But he *didn't* arrest us," Lizzie repeated.

Bootsie smiled slyly. "Jim isn't going to throw his Snuggle Bug into jail. Besides, he doesn't have any spare cells. The two holding cells at the police station are currently occupied. At least until Madame Flora and her husband are transferred to Indy. The state prosecutor is taking over the case. They face a murder charge, remember?"

"Snuggle Bug?" said Lizzie. Unable to hide her amusement.

Bootsie giggled. "Don't you and Edgar have pet names?"

"He calls me Red," Lizzie admitted. "And lately I call him Sasquatch." With his shaggy hair and bushy beard, Edgar no longer looked the part of a clean-cut bank president. He did look a bit like a swamp monster. He was enjoying his retirement, fishing with Beau and hiking along the Wabash.

Everybody laughed at these fanciful appellations.

"Ben calls me Carnac the Magnificent," confessed Cookie. "Because of my memory thing."

"That was the skit Johnny Carson used to do about a 'mystic from the East' who could psychically divine unknown answers to unseen questions," Maddy explained to the younger members of the group. She and Beau used to watch

Johnny Carson every night. But Jimmy Fallon was too "young" for their tastes.

"Right," nodded Cookie. "And I call him Torog."

"Hey, that's the Elven name for trolls in *Lord of the Rings*," said N'yen, a big J.R.R. Tolkien fan. Not that the boy was into fantasy, just that he liked to play the computer games. Among his favorites were *The Hobbit, Battle for Middle Earth II*, and *Return of the King*.

"That's because he's so short and stout, just like a troll," Cookie said, affection evident in her voice. "Nothing like a werewolf," she added, glancing at Maddy as a rebuke to her aunts.

"How about you, Maddy?" prodded Bootsie. Looking for more pet names to disguise her own embarrassment. Snuggle Bug, indeed!

"Beau? I call him my Pooh Bear."

"And what does he call you?" pressed Lizzie.

"I'd rather not say."

"C'mon, you're among friends – your best-est friends," nudged Bootsie.

Maddy blushed. "He calls me his Honey Pot. You see, Pooh Bear likes –"

"Honey," Cookie completed the sentence. "We know the story of Winnie-the-Pooh."

"Oooo," Aggie made a face. "TMI – Too Much Information," she squealed.

"What's the big deal?" asked N'yen, not getting the sexual innuendo. "I've read all the Pooh books by A.A. Milne. Winnie was always looking for a Honey Pot."

"I've read them too," said Sissy. Trying to impress N'yen with her reading habits. "I always liked Tigger best. My cat Mittens reminds me of Tigger. He's an orange tabby, the same color."

Maddy tried to get the subject off her pet name. "Who's going to check with Suzy Q about her ancestor, Archie Aitkens?" she asked.

"You go," suggested Lizzie. "She likes you. And take Bootsie with you. Petie used to be one of Jim's deputies, so he trusts her."

Maddy said, "I think Cookie should go too. She knows the Aitkens family tree. She can connect Archibald Aikens to Suzy, generation by generation.

"Good point," agreed Lizzie.

"Maybe we all should go," said Cookie.

"Me too?" asked Aggie.

"Dear, stay here with me," smiled Leslie Ann. "My husband is coming up from Indy today. I'd like you to be here with me to greet him. I want to show off my friends."

"Meet the Earl of Greystone?"

"Oliver to you, dear."

"Okay," she agreed. "Can N'yen and Sissy meet him too?"

"Of course, if they'd like."

"My chance to meet royalty?" gushed Sissy. "You bet!"

"You've met Leslie Ann," corrected N'yen. "Technically, she's royalty."

"Oh, countesses are a dime a dozen. But I'm honored to be an auxiliary member of the Quilters Club. I still sew quilts, you know."

"Come along," Maddy said to her besties. "I'll drive."

"It's a longshot they know anything," Cookie warned them. "Remember, Suzy Q was Floyd Aitkens' long-lost daughter. Nobody even knew about her until a couple of years ago. She hasn't had much connection with the Aitkens family before inheriting the watermelon farm."

"Then she gave it all away and married Petie," Bootsie completed the story. "It was quite a romance."

"Was her long-ago ancestor, Archibald Aitkens, a fat redheaded farmer like the Count's letter said?" asked Lizzie. Being a redhead herself, this detail fascinated her.

"That information is lost to history," said Cookie with a shrug. "But Suzy Q's great-uncle Rufus was likely a redhead. His nickname was 'Ginger,' according to old records. That's a pretty good clue."

~ ~ ~

Old McDonald's had a contract to supply milk for Sealtest, but it still carried a number of local customers on the books. The dairy farm delivered rattling bottles of pasteurized milk in metal carriers, left in insulated tin boxes next to the doorstop. Petie oversaw the cows and the milking machines; Susy managed the delivery trucks. Under their management, the number of employees had doubled. Business was good.

A paved driveway with green pastures on both sides led up to the white farmhouse. The large red milking barn lay in the distance. Herds of Jersey cattle milled in the surrounding pastures, grazing on the luxuriant ryegrass.

Jerseys are a favorite milk cow. Known as "The Little Beauties," these cows are a smaller breed, with soft brown hair and big beautiful eyes. Jersey milk tends to be a bit creamier. It's 18% higher in protein, 20% higher in calcium, and with 25% more butterfat than "standard" milk. And it's also rich in essential vitamins and minerals such as zinc, iodine and vitamins A, B, D, and E. Naturally sweet, Jersey milk also makes good ice cream.

The Hitzers' farmhouse with its shiny tin roof and shady wrap-around porch looked like a painting by Grandma Moses. As Bootsie and Maddy and Lizzie and Cookie stood there on the porch, they were amused that the doorbell played a tinny version of "*Old McDonald had a farm, E-I-E-I-O.*"

Susan Quinlan Aitkens Hitzer answered the door, a big smile to greet them. Her emerald-green eyes and tousled black hair were striking, like a county fair beauty queen. "Bootsie! Maddy! Lizzie! Cookie! Do come in," she held the door wide as she ushered her visitors inside.

"Hi, Suzy. Is Petie home?" Bootsie opened the conversation.

"He's down at the barn. One of the milking machines is broken. He's swapping it out with a new one. Facing retirement, his parents let a lot of the equipment go without proper upkeep. Can't say as I blame them. They didn't know that Petie was willing to take over the farm. I talked him into it. I like raising cows better than plowing watermelon fields. I understand the co-op I set up is working out well for the town."

"Yes," said Maddy, speaking as the mother-in-law of the mayor. "It's certainly helping the town's beleaguered budget. Our recovery from that 2018 tornado is almost complete."

"Thanks to your aunt's generous contribution."

"And yours – with the watermelon co-op."

Suzy Q smiled modestly. "Don't tell anybody, but I have a watermelon allergy. That would be heresy in the watermelon capitol of Indiana. I thought it best to get out of the melon farming business."

"Your secret is safe with us," said Lizzie. A dubious promise, knowing her propensity for gossip.

"Ditto," said Bootsie, mimicking zipping her lips.

Suzy waved their protestations away. "No big deal. It's a medical condition, that's all."

"But you have to admit it's a bit ironic, the heir to the largest watermelon farm in the county allergic to watermelons," Maddy observed.

"Yes, I suppose it is. What brings you ladies out to the dairy? Need some milk for an ice cream social?"

"No," Cookie spoke up. "It has to do with one of your ancestors."

"My ancestors? I know very little about them, especially on the Aitkens side. As you know, I was Floyd's secret love child, hidden away from the family most of my life."

Cookie smiled reassuringly. "I understand, but we need to ask if you've ever heard of an ancestor named Archibald Reginald Aitkens?"

"No, I don't recognize the name."

"He was your great-great-grandfather," Bootsie explained. "We think a Count Antonio Guicciardini gave him a package to hold, but the Count was killed in a duel and never retrieved it."

"And you think I might have it, handed down from my father?"

"I know you do," said Maddy.

"What makes you so positive?"

"This," Maddy pointed to a framed wall handing over the couch in the living room. About 2 ½-feet by 4-feet, it was a piece of brown fabric with illustrated panels, scenes of a knight doing battle against a man wearing a crown – Sir Tristan vying with King Mark of Cornwell for the love of Isolde.

"Oh that. It was in a trunk in the attic at the old Aitkens homeplace. I thought it was kinda interesting, so I had it framed to spice up this place. Petie's mother favored black velvet paintings of the Last Supper. The house needed a little makeover." She smiled meekly, then added, "No offense if any of you like black velvet."

"No worry there," said Lizzie. She preferred Thomas Kincaid "light" paintings.

"Not at all," agreed Bootsie. Her main decoration being a picture of dogs playing poker.

Cookie kept her own counsel, but she was a Norman Rockwell aficionado. The reproductions on her living room walls were very high end, right down to the brush strokes.

She'd heard that the Rockwell paintings on the walls at *The Saturday Evening Post* were actually reproductions, the real paintings locked away in a storage area for security.

Maddy was surrounded in the Mansion by lots of valuable oils in gilded frames, mostly Hoosier Group paintings by T.C. Steel, Richard Gruelle, William Forsyth, I. Otis Adams, and Otto Stark. These 19th-Century Indiana impressionists were noted for their landscapes. But she most valued her husband's copies of them, a hobby that made him happy.

"Is this what that Count left with Archibald Aitkens?" asked Suzy Q, examining the wall-hanging as if seeing it for the first time.

Lizzie stepped forward to give the fabric her own once-over. "Yes," she said, the awe apparent in her voice, "I believe it is."

"Is it valuable?"

"Very."

Chapter Thirty-Six

Prince Charming

Oliver Trent, the Earl of Greystone, was as handsome as a Disney Prince. And Leslie Ann Trent made a perfect complement, like the couple atop a wedding cake.

"I am so happy to finally meet you," the Earl bowed to Maddy and Beau, "– my wife's second family."

"She's very dear to us," replied Maddy.

"And to me," smiled the Earl.

"Hush, all of you," said Leslie Ann. "You're embarrassing me."

"You must come visit us," continued the Earl of Greystone.

"Yes, our home has 14 bedrooms," laughed Leslie Ann. "Plenty of room for everyone."

"Fourteen bedrooms," exclaimed N'yen. "Do you live in a castle?"

"A small one," he admitted. "But nothing as elaborate as the Hoople Mansion. You live in a castle yourself."

"Thank you," said Maddy. "It belongs to my aunts."

Oliver said, "I understand you ladies – the Quilters Club – found another fragment of the Tristan and Isolde Quilt?"

"We did," Aggie declared. "But Leslie Ann –uh, Lady Greystone – helped us."

"I am friendly with the curator at the Victoria and Albert Museum. If you like, I can arrange to reunite your fragment with the piece of the quilt they already have."

"Thanks for the offer, My Lord," curtsied Lizzie, perhaps overdoing it. "But this part of the Tristan Quilt has a home here in the Hoople Quilting Heritage Museum. After all, it's been a part of this community for nearly two hundred years."

"But how can you claim it? A representative of the Guicciardini family may have left it in the care of a local friend, but this is not finders keepers. I'm sure the V&A will be happy to purchase it from the Guicciardinis."

"Oh, it's too late, my dearest," Leslie Ann soothed her husband.

"Too late? How?"

"I'm afraid I'm to blame. I phoned the heir of Mario Guicciardini, the man to whom the quilt was being sent. Dr. Jonathan Guicciardini has agreed to donate this portion of the Tristan Quilt to Quilting Heritage Museum."

"Why would he do that?"

"Me, dearest. He likes my British accent."

Chapter Thirty-Seven

The Ring

Beau Madison was relieved to find out that his ancestor – one of the august Founding Fathers of Caruthers Corners – had not faced an actual werewolf. That wolf-man monsters were the thing old Universal horror movies.

He'd known that all along, of course. But those hand-me-down stories about Col. Beauregard Madison and the silver bullet were somewhat disconcerting. It was calming to discover that Count Guicciardini's strange behavior had a rational explanation.

Rabies.

This zoonotic, viral disease is fairly rare in the US, only 1 to 3 cases a year. But worldwide an estimated 59,000 people die from the bite of a rabid animal – a dog, a bat, or whatever – each year.

Whether N'yen would pass along the story to his future son would be up to him. Now that it had been explained, the story seemed to have less significance. But Beau Madison had done his duty, passed the story along, and that was the end of it for him.

Beau gave the box containing the "silver bullet" – his great-grandfathers wedding ring – to the boy. "Here," he said. "This is yours now. But instead of passing it along, I'd suggest you turn it back to its original form. When the time comes you get married, melt it down and have it made into a wedding ring."

"Gee, Grampy, that's a long way off. I'm only sixteen. And Sissy and I aren't even dating yet."

"Time will come," smiled the old man.

Epilogue

Stitching It All Together

Caruthers Corners returned to normal. Well, sort of.

The Tristan Quilt became a permanent exhibit at the Hoople Quilting Heritage Museum. Lizzie Ridenour was so proud of the acquisition, hanging there next to the Renaissance Quilt. There was a special opening that feted Susan Aitkens for preserving the fragment of the Tristan Quilt. And the Hoople Quadruplets Trust Fund flew in Dr. Jonathan Guicciardini to celebrate his generous donation. He was disappointed that Leslie Ann wasn't there.

Lord and Lady Greystone had returned to London where the Earl promptly got involved in politics – something to do with Brexit. The Countess started a fundraiser to build a quilting museum in the East Kensington district of London. Sticking to her Quilters Club roots.

Shortly after that, Billy Hofstadter bought the T-Mobile store and announced his engagement to Frances Morgan. He said it was time to settle down.

Heinrich Bashinski got a life sentence at Indiana State Prison. His wife Florence is doing ten years (as an accessory) at the Rockville Correctional Facility.

Chief Jim Purdue promoted Harry Teague to Head Detective. It came with a pay raise. Jim had found his eventual successor of chief of police.

The late Robert Bob Roberts left his business to his son Bobby. The boy had no idea what to do with three rooms piled high with books, rare manuscripts, autographs, and antique photographs. Cookie Bentley had made an appointment to cull through the artifacts for any pieces having to do with local history. Maddy had offered the Caruthers Corners Historical

Society a grant to purchase any relevant books or documents.

Aggie Tidemore made the Dean's list her second semester at Yale. Bobby Elwood proposed when she was home on Christmas break, but she turned him down. She wanted to complete her education before settling down to a house with a white picket fence. Or even a great stone castle high on a hill.

N'yen Madison discovered a new quasar and there was talk about naming it after him, the youngest astrophysicist to find one. Quasars are remote celestial objects that contain massive black holes and may represent a stage in the evolution of some galaxies. While more than a million quasars have been observed, only a handful have received proper names – The Einstein Cross, Cloverleaf, Teacup Galaxy, etc. – as opposed to a coded designation from a survey, catalog or list. N'yen was making quite a name for himself at Northwestern's Dearborn Observatory. And perhaps in the stars.

Cecelia LaToya Jackson won a regional quilting award – The Golden Needle – for her unique variation on a Jelly Roll Twist Quilt. Instead of using pre-cut 2 ½-inch strips of fabric cut from selvage to selvage, she had doubled the size to turn it into a magnificent wall hanging. Lizzie was proud of her new protégé.

Bootsie Purdue brought three more dogs home from the shelter, a scrappy lot of unadoptable pooches that she named Yabba, Dabba, and Doo. She already had one dog named Doo, but that didn't stop her redundant nomenclature. Her husband Jim was just happy to have her – and her Quilters Club cronies – out of his hair (had he had any).

Ben Bentley was no longer speaking to the Hoople sisters. Not so much because of the water in the face, but because he was insulted to be called a werewolf.

His wife Cookie is still telling the story of Hilda and Helga Hoople's visit, a Mason jar of Holy Water in hand. She can't tell it with a straight face. She said she was thankful Ben hadn't melted into a puddle like the witch in *The Wizard of Oz*.

Aunt Hilda and Aunt Helga sent a note of apology to Ben Bentley, but they weren't sincere. They still believed werewolves inhabited the town, posing as normal folk until the call of a full moon. But they weren't concerned. They still had two gallons of Holy Water stashed in the closet next to the front door. They hoped their splash of Holy Water had broken Ben Bentley's werewolf spell.

Beau Madison could rest easy. He had satisfied the requirements of his family tradition, passing on the story of Col. Madison and the werewolf – along with the "silver bullet" – to a descendant. What N'yen chose to do with this was up to him. Sometimes Beau thought his wife Maddy was right, that the present time is more important than the past.

As for Maddy, she turned her attention back to quiltmaking and baking Watermelon Upside Down cakes and keeping up with her grandchildren. Little Donna Ann (Freddie's daughter) was spending more and more time at the Hoople Mansion, whooping and hollering like Red Injuns with her cousins, Aggie's sisters known as the "Trio of Trouble." She loved it.

Needless to say, Maddy's daughter Tilly was upset to learn that Madame Flora was a fraud and that there was no spirit guide to help her explore the Other Side. But she moved on, getting involved in New Age crystal power.

In fact, she got trapped in an offshoot of the Crystal Palace in Marengo Cave, a US National Natural Landmark in Southern Indiana. But how she got there and how she escaped from "ravenous killer Morlocks" hiding in the cavern is a story for another time.

Thank you for reading.
Please review this book. Reviews
help others find Absolutely Amazing eBooks and
inspire us to keep providing these marvelous tales.
If you would like to be put on our email list
to receive updates on new releases,
contests, and promotions, please go to
AbsolutelyAmazingEbooks.com and sign up.

About The Author

MARJORY SORRELL ROCKWELL says needlecraft arts – quilting, crocheting, knitting – are pastimes every woman can appreciate. And she particularly loves quiltmaking. "It's like painting with cloth," she says. But when not quilting she writes mysteries about a Midwestern sleuth not unlike herself, a middle-aged lady with an unpredictable family and loyal friends. And she's a big fan of watermelon pie.

ABSOLUTELY AMAZING eBOOKS

AbsolutelyAmazingeBooks.com
or AA-eBooks.com